Empyrea
and Other Stories

Carrie Gessner

To Elphie, who makes me smile

Contents

Thank you to:

Aradia Publishing, Cloaked Press, *Freeze Frame Fiction*, *The Future Fire*, Left Hand Publishers, and Sez Publishing for giving some of these stories their very first place to live.

My favorite authors, who give me stories and characters to love and ponder and whose writing makes me strive to improve.

My writing community, which is now *so* big. I'm awed and grateful every day.

My friends, who let me talk about writing without ever complaining about how *much* I talk about writing.

As always, special thanks to my family for all the support.

Empyrea

Niyah leaned forward in the saddle to pat her horse's neck. "Just a little farther, girl."

She'd hit the dark side of the world an hour ago, and the guards wouldn't follow her here. They were too scared to, and yet the thumping of her heart was still loud and fast enough that she couldn't slow down. Not yet.

She finally did when the plains were broken by the forest. Her eyes had adjusted to the darkness, but that didn't mean she could see well enough to lead her horse. She hadn't escaped only to have her neck broken being thrown from the saddle.

As they picked their way among trunks and over roots, Niyah willed her breathing to calm. She was all right. She was safe now. Even if she had no plan beyond her escape, she was safe.

"Halt!"

The voice preceded a beam of light shining directly in her face. She squinted and threw an arm in front of her eyes to protect them.

Then rough hands grabbed her elbows and wrenched her off the saddle and onto the ground, onto her knees. Her eyes watered from a light source shoved near her head.

She was wrong to come here. She was an outsider. Why should they like outsiders any more than her own people did?

"Gentle now," said another voice, softer and slightly higher. "You're scaring her. And get the lantern out of her face."

The light receded, and the hands released her, and Niyah wiped at her eyes to clear them of tears. As she squinted, the shadow in front of her resolved into the figure of a woman whose skin was so pale it shone in the moonlight.

The woman's smile was kind. "It's all right. You're all right. Yeah?"

Niyah gave a shaky nod. It seemed like what the woman wanted from her.

"Good. My name's Gesa."

Niyah, licking lips dry with fear, looked around at the three others nearby. All, including this woman, looked like soldiers. Would they hurt her?

"It seems pretty clear," Gesa said, "but you came from the Light, didn't you?"

Again, Niyah nodded.

"Good. Are you running from something? From someone?"

This time, Niyah chanced her voice. "Yes."

"Well," Gesa said, her expression soft, "you need run no longer." She helped Niyah to her feet and added, "But we have to take you to the governor."

What would the governor do to her? Would he punish her like she would've been punished in her own land? Had she escaped one hell only to exchange it for another?

Gesa must have seen the fear on her face because she put gentle hands on Niyah's arms. "It's nothing to worry about. We just want to know how long you're staying, whether you need a roof to sleep under, when the last time was you ate. That sort of thing. We'll take care of you. You can leave whenever you wish."

Niyah wasn't so sure about that, but she let Gesa hand her the reins to her horse and lead her and the other guards eastward. What else was she to do?

Her horse wasn't like theirs. Just as Niyah's skin was darker, so was her mare's coat, as black as her fierce eyes and complemented by a silver mane. The combination gave her an ethereality that seemed to spook the guards.

Niyah kept her mind blank as they walked, for it would do no good to worry. The trek into the settlement was short, short enough that even if the guards hadn't found her, she would've reached it on her own soon enough.

The village was composed of long buildings made of wattle and daub and frames of thick lumber. Between the buildings, packed-dirt lanes ran in neat lines, lighted by skinny poles stuck in the ground with torches on top. For a settlement in the Nightlands, it was surprisingly bright.

The other guards took the horses toward stables that lay at the town's southern edge. Niyah relinquished her reins only after a reassurance from Gesa that the mare would be well taken care of.

Then Gesa led her toward the middle of the village and knocked upon the door of a modest dwelling adjacent to a public square.

After a heartbeat, the door opened to reveal a woman who was a little taller than Niyah, with dark hair that cascaded over her shoulders; sharp, intelligent eyes; and pale skin, just like Gesa's. Just like everyone else's in the Nightlands. After all, they never saw the sun.

"Gesa," the woman said with a smile. "Come in. And you've brought a guest."

Niyah stepped inside and looked around as Gesa conversed quietly with the woman. The dwelling's interior was lighted by torches along the walls and a central fire in a stone pit. On her right was a table laid with food and drink. One wall was lined with alcoves that looked to be sleeping areas, and a staircase to the left led to a second story. Warmth permeated the room, and not just because of the fire.

But there was no evidence of other people. Did the woman live alone? If Niyah had been able to do that, if she had been afforded some solitude, would her life have turned out differently?

The conversation reached her ears just as Gesa addressed the woman by title.

Niyah abruptly faced the stranger. "You're the governor?" The words stuttered out of her mouth before she could stop them.

The woman raised an eyebrow, but she seemed more amused than annoyed. "That's right. My name is Emery. What's yours?"

"Niyah."

"Well, Niyah, please," said Emery, extending a hand toward the table. "Sit. Eat. You do eat, do you not?"

Niyah managed a nod. This woman was different from what she'd expected. She hadn't expected a woman at all. Things were so strange here in the Nightlands.

Perhaps not in a bad way, though.

Gesa left, and Emery sat at the table.

She took a bite of meat, followed it with a long sip of her drink, and gestured at the surrounding room. "You may sit and eat or warm yourself by the fire or go to sleep. Whatever pleases you."

Whatever pleased her? No one had ever asked what pleased Niyah before. She swallowed thickly. "What would you like me to do?"

Emery paused for only a second as she dipped a chunk of bread in a bowl of steaming soup. "I should like to talk to you, but only if you should like to talk to me."

Niyah sat on the bench across the table from Emery, who poured her a cup of something reddish and strong-smelling. Niyah let it be, but at Emery's urging, she took a small loaf of bread.

"Gesa said that you'd been running, that you'd been frightened," said Emery. "Would you like to tell me what has you so frightened?"

Niyah tore off a piece of bread and chewed it slowly. Once she swallowed, she said, "My people. I . . . I've been exiled."

Not quite a lie. She had exiled herself in order to save herself from the stake.

The governor's expression didn't change, but her dark eyes flashed. With a warning? Or with something else? "Why?"

This could go very badly, but Niyah couldn't outrun the truth forever, even if it cost her her safety.

She dropped her gaze to the table, almost mesmerized by the pattern of the grain. "I killed a man."

"With premeditation or in self-defense?"

"What?" Though they spoke a common language, the question made no sense.

Emery set down her cup. "Did you plan to kill this man?"

"No."

"Then it happened in the heat of the moment?"

Niyah closed her eyes against the memory. But the governor needed an answer. "Yes."

"Did you attack him without provocation?"

"No."

"Then he provoked you? Threatened you even?"

Niyah bit her bottom lip. It didn't matter, did it? The way? The only thing that mattered was that she, a woman, stepped out of her place and killed a man.

"You don't have to tell me," said Emery, her voice soft. "But I think it would help if you did."

Niyah sipped the wine provided to fortify herself. "My husband was . . . a violent man."

Emery hummed. "He beat you?"

Niyah gave a hesitant nod. Even when the bruises that marred her skin faded, she would still bear invisible scars.

Emery sat back with a sigh. "And for this, your people exiled you?"

"Would not your people do the same?" Niyah asked.

"No," Emery said sadly. "We would call you brave." She swirled the liquid in her cup and seemed faraway.

Brave had never been a word attributed to Niyah. *Empty-headed. Worthless. Pitiful.* Never *brave*. It was enough to bring her to the verge of tears. Instead of allowing them to fall, she took small bites of bread to distract herself. Not for the first time, she wondered what sort of land this was—and whether she could ever belong in such a place.

Emery cleared her throat. "Forgive me. I was lost in thought. I'd like to know more about you and where you come from. Will you tell me what you do?"

"I don't understand."

"What are your skills? Do you perform labor of any sort in order to feed yourself, your family?"

"Oh." Niyah flexed her hands. As a woman, she'd been encouraged to do what her father and brothers told her to, and they'd told her that the thing she loved most in the world was useless.

But the woman sitting opposite regarded her with intelligent, sympathetic eyes. Would she say the same thing?

Niyah straightened her shoulders. "I'm an artist."

The governor's face softened. "An artist? The province could always use more of those."

"It could?"

"Artists think differently than other people do. Actually, just being from the Light means you think differently than anyone in this village does. And the more perspectives we have, the better we are at building a community."

Again, heat welled behind Niyah's eyes. Was it possible she'd stumbled upon a place where she'd be valued? It was almost too good to believe.

"There are tales of people from your land coming to mine or people from mine going to yours—more recently than our common ancestors, of course—but I thought that was all they were. Tales," Emery said with a smile. "I'd hoped it would happen in my lifetime, though, and since this province is at the edge of our lands, at the edge of the division, I thought we had the best chance of anyone. I'm glad that turned out to be true."

"Why?"

"Niyah," Emery said kindly, "you've made an extraordinary journey. You will have to adapt much like our ancestors did. It won't be easy to live in constant darkness. The darkness has her challenges, and she is not forgiving, but, should you like to stay, we will teach you how to navigate her shadows." She peeled the blue rind of an unfamiliar fruit. "You, in turn, have much to teach us."

Niyah scoffed. What could she teach the governor?

"You don't believe me, and if I've guessed your situation well enough, that's to be expected. Right now, you need rest. Perhaps you'll feel differently in the morning." Emery rose and went to stand in front of one of the alcoves in the wall. "This bed is closest to the fire, and I've left some extra blankets, as well."

Arms crossed protectively over her torso, Niyah followed her host. "I can stay?"

"For as long as you like. In the morning, I could take you around the village, show you how we live if that's something you desire."

"I think . . . I do."

Emery nodded. "Then goodnight. I sleep upstairs, but if you need anything in the night, don't hesitate to wake me."

It wasn't until Emery had a foot on the staircase in the corner that Niyah asked, "Why are you being so kind to me?"

Emery turned, a frown gracing her lips, and gazed at her for a long moment. "What is your land like that you've never experienced kindness?"

As cruel as the sun that lights it.

Before Niyah could speak the words, Emery smiled and softly said, "Rest now. We will talk in the morning."

Morning without sunlight. An odd concept, foreign, but not unwelcome. Niyah had always assumed darkness would be cold. Instead, it seemed to wrap her in a gentle, protective embrace.

Emery provided her with food to break their fast and, once they ate, beckoned Niyah outside to show her the village.

She made it only a few steps from the door. Torches bathed the village in soft light, much like the previous night, but it was the sky that caught her attention.

Thousands—millions?—of pinpricks of silver dotted the inky sky, like tiny lanterns shining down upon her. Under their light, though it was feeble, Niyah didn't feel so alone. Under their light, the night wasn't so frightening after all.

"I forgot," Emery said, "that you have never seen the night sky."

"What are they?" Niyah breathed, her chest full of warmth and something close to hope.

"They're suns."

Niyah turned to her companion. "No. These are no suns." They were nothing like the one that blazed upon her land.

"They are. They're simply much farther away than the one you know." Emery stared at her intently for a long moment before she said, "I have an idea. Come with me?"

"Where?"

The governor's eyes sparkled. "I want to introduce you to someone who might be able to make use of your talents."

Niyah followed, glancing up every few steps to marvel. Would she ever get used to this?

At the northern edge of the village sat a tower that stretched three stories over the other buildings. Emery led her inside and then up, up to the highest floor.

A woman with short white hair turned at their entrance. She stood in front of a long tubular contraption. Niyah couldn't begin to guess at its purpose.

"Margret," Emery said.

Margret's smile creased her face, and she embraced the governor. "Always a pleasure to see you, Emery, when your duties allow you a spare moment. And who might this be?"

"This is Niyah. Niyah, meet Margret," the governor said, waving a hand between them.

"Welcome, Niyah."

Her smile was so hospitable that Niyah returned it without thought. "Thank you."

"Now, Governor," Margret said, "not that I don't value a visit from you, but I assume you're here for my help. How may I be of service?"

"Actually," Emery said, "I thought Niyah here might be able to help *you*."

"Oh?"

Niyah looked between the two women. While Margret seemed curious, Emery looked almost . . . proud.

"I-I'm an artist," said Niyah.

Margret's face brightened. "Is that so? Come over here. Come, come."

And with a hand on Niyah's shoulders, she directed her to the contraption at the back of the room. It stuck out through the window, whose shutters were thrown open, and pointed toward the sky.

Margret tapped a small circular piece. "Look through here and tell me what you see."

Niyah bent her head. Only one eye fit against the glass, so she had to close the other for the picture to resolve. When it did, the night sky appeared, and her breath caught.

"The suns Emery told me about," she said in awe. "Only they seem bigger through here. Much bigger."

"That's right," Margret said. "We call them stars, and this device is called a telescope. It magnifies them so I may study them."

Niyah straightened in surprise. "You study them?"

If Margret lived in the Light, she would've been banished—at the best—for even thinking such a blasphemy. But here in the Nightlands, she studied. She learned. And Niyah's chest nearly burst when she realized that she, too, could do the same. No longer would she been seen as troublesome or useless.

"That's right," Margret said. "I chart them, chart their movements in the sky. The only thing is I'm rubbish at drawing. And who ever heard of a mapmaker who couldn't draw?"

Emery grinned, and Niyah finally understood what her plan had been.

Niyah, too excited to speak, licked her lips. Then she said, "I can draw. I can paint, too."

"Well, then, that seems to fit very prettily, doesn't it?" Margret said. "Should you like to work with me, to be my apprentice?"

Niyah blinked. She should've expected it, but the fact that she had a choice in the matter still took her aback. For once, she would have a say in how she got to live her day-to-day life without being told to stay in her place, a place that had felt so much like a cage.

"How about it, Niyah?" Emery asked.

"Yes!" Her cheeks went hot at the others' laughter, but it was kind laughter. "Yes, I should like that very much."

"Then it's settled! I will leave you two to get acquainted," said Emery. "Niyah, Margret will escort you to my house when you're finished for the day. You'll sup with me and sleep there again. Tomorrow's our day of rest, so I'll show you the village then, introduce you, and we can find you a more permanent place to live."

Niyah didn't reply. She couldn't or else she would begin to cry. Her expression must have been thanks enough, for the governor took her leave and Margret put an arm around Niyah's shoulders.

"We have a lot to learn, you and I, and I can't wait to get started," Margret said. She bustled Niyah toward the drawing table in the center of the room. "Sit, sit."

Margret set papers, pens, inks, brushes, and paints before her. These were followed by books, piles of books with which she would learn about the sky.

About the stars.

When she looked up from the tools of her education and caught the smile on her new teacher's face, Niyah finally understood what it was to be free.

The Offerings

In the early years, the gifts match your age. The night you turn one, Mama instructs you to sleep with your favorite blankie clasped in your tiny fist.

"Don't let go," she chastises. "Don't you ever let go."

You sleep because you don't understand—not yet, not for a few years more—and when you wake, the blanket is gone and the clock:

three hundred sixty-four days

sixteen hours

twenty-one minutes

forty-seven seconds

In the early years, the gifts match your age. Your rocking horse on which you pretend to be a cowboy, lassoing your pillows. Your stuffed octopus with its swirly limbs that wrap around you, usher you into dreamless sleep. Your favorite book of fairy tales, the gruesome ones you insist Mama reads though they fill your head with nightmares. Always things you'd rather keep, but not as much as your life.

In the adolescent years, the gifts get strange, awkward like you as you push the limits of what will keep you alive for one more year. You offer your outsized retainer, whose impression remains in your perfect teeth. Your cellphone, so precious you know you *have* to give it up. Your history paper, your first B after nine years of As, the one you'll always keep in your head as a reminder to work harder. As long as it's a piece of yourself, one you hold dear, the offer cannot be rejected.

In your twenties, the gifts become personal. Your hand-annotated copy of *I Capture The Castle*, spine broken, pages spilling out because you read it twelve times after your first heartbreak. Your daddy's watch, overlarge, stopped at half-past four, a comfort on your freckled wrist. Your picture strip of you and your best friend from a carnival photobooth, heads thrown back in laughter.

You're twenty-eight the night you chance it, three decades of Mama's warnings ringing in your brain. "Early to bed, late to rise, and never, never open your eyes." Immortal knowledge is not for mortals to seek, but this year you do it because you're adrift and what could you lose?

You slip under the covers without undressing and hold onto the wooden plane that represents all the things you never became. You wanted to be a pilot until your eyes forced you into thick glasses and your seventh-grade teacher convinced you girls couldn't do math. So you gave up on flying. You gave up on dreaming.

You're shaking with the sorrow of lost potential when it appears as a glimmer that resolves into a human figure, into a woman, confusion in her eyes.

"You're not supposed to be awake," she says.

"I wanted to know."

Confusion sparks into curiosity. "Know what?"

"Whether it's worth it."

"Every life is worth it."

You don't believe it. You *can't* believe it. There's nothing worthy about living without family, dreams, hopes. You've lost your way, and you don't know how to ask for it back.

You spend the next year waiting for your twenty-ninth birthday. You go to work, eat, sleep, sometimes read. When coworkers ask you out for drinks, you make excuses until they stop asking. When the night arrives, you hold a book in your lap and stare at the same page until she comes.

"This isn't living," she says.

"I know." You know and yet you have no desire to change. You can find no value in this rundown apartment, the fridge that keeps breaking, the stale smell of cigarettes that won't come out. You can find no value in endless labor.

"Why should I accept your offering?" she asks.

"If it's a true one, you're not allowed to refuse."

She purses her lips and crosses her arms and waits for the offering.

You hold out the book. Imagination. In this dull life, your most precious commodity.

Her eyes narrow. She knows this, and because she knows, she doesn't ask. Instead: "What will you give me next year?"

"I thought it was supposed to be a surprise."

She smirks—an honest-to-goodness smirk. "I'm allowed to guess, but you never give me what I expect."

"Well, perhaps I won't have anything to give at all."

"Don't," she says.

And every night for the next year, you dream of this one, the word echoing in your cavernous chest until its murmur resonates at the same frequency as your bones.

The night you turn thirty, you don't even pretend to sleep. You sit against the headboard, a mug of tea in your hand, and wait for the person who has become your reason for staying alive.

She smiles for the first time in your brief acquaintance and greets you with a wry, "How surprising it is to find you awake."

You think you're friends enough not to have to stifle your chuckle. If she hasn't gotten you in trouble the past two years, she won't start now. She'll keep this secret in her life like you keep it in yours.

Beneath her breath: "The things mortals do for forever."

"I don't want forever," you say, not realizing the truth of it until it slips out.

"Then what is it you want?" she asks.

You cannot answer. You cannot answer, and so she takes your mug and the comfort it symbolizes and disappears for another year.

Thirty-one.

Her smile is small, gaze focused on your empty hands. "You have nothing for me."

"Not true. You asked me what it was I wanted. It's taken me a year, but I have the answer now."

She sits on the blanket at the foot of your bed and waits, patience in tangible form. You wish you hadn't spent the last

three hundred

sixty-five

days

feeling like your skeleton was vibrating right out of your skin. Now, your whole being is still.

"My offering is that I'll take something from you."

And she is quiet for so long you think you may have accidentally stolen her voice.

When finally she speaks, the question that surfaces is:

"Will you take my loneliness?"

Creatures of the Night Shift

Dannie shifts into a more comfortable reading position—legs over the back of the armchair, head hanging over the seat edge. In her hands is Carmilla, a little light research, something she meant to finish in her old life. Stoker and Rice sit on her 'read' pile, along with some nonfiction titles and even a poetry collection. By now, the books are more humorous than helpful.

Though her bedroom door is closed, it doesn't keep out all the noise her sisters are making downstairs—banging around in the kitchen, arguing more than talking, probably wrestling, too.

Seven forty-nine AM. Positively late-night by vampire family standards. If only they would shut the hell up for a while.

All things considered, life at twenty-five and one week sucks about the same as life at twenty-four. Well, literally, it sucks just a bit more. She still hasn't gotten the hang of this vampire thing. Her life is full of all the things it used to be full of—a crappy job at the local library, trips to the bookstore, late-night walks in the park, an ever-expanding tea collection. Despite the faded week-old bites on her neck, she feels more human than ever, right down to her shitty taste in pop music.

She *did* have to switch to the night shift. Work is a hellhole no matter what time of day, but at least her bosses aren't there after six PM.

Horace isn't there, either, though.

She grinds the heels of her hands into her closed eyes. A good way to stop thinking about her crush is to imagine him at dinner with her family—two parents, four older sisters, all creatures of the night.

Hell, she's terrible at this. All of her sisters had gotten it in, like, the first hour of undeadness. It's not fair, really. They were beautiful and athletic and talented and amazeballs without the family gift (or curse, however you want to look at it), and they only got more so. She's the baby, the one always a few steps behind, the one who always needs to be taken care of.

Sam, Alex, Jo, and Charley are great sisters, really. In the past week alone, they've taken her to parties, introduced her to their friends, brought her into the community. They're well-intentioned, but can't just one sister be not quite perfect? It was supposed to be different after she turned, but she's still just clumsy little Dannie. Still average. Still almost human save for the fangs and the appetite change. God, they're going to tease her mercilessly when they find out she's crushing on a human.

A *thud* from downstairs, followed by heavy, fast footsteps.

Exasperated, Dannie sits up and shouts, "What the hell, guys? Are you racing in steel-toed boots down there?"

She scoffs and settles right-side up, but her book is no longer an adequate distraction.

"Dannie dearest! Lovely youngest sister of mine!"

It's Alex, the second oldest, who is tall and gorgeous and everything Dannie wants to grow up to be. Only there won't be any more growing up. She's stuck forever at twenty-five.

But she could get used to that, right?

She'll *have* to get used to it.

"Hey, kiddo!" Alex calls up the staircase. "Someone's here to see you!"

Dannie groans. There's no one on the planet she wants to see right now, except for maybe her parents. But work keeps them busy, too, and they're big into smothering on a schedule, which means Saturday morning breakfasts and holiday feasts and turning rituals.

Dannie tosses her book onto the bed and traipses down the stairs. Alex stands on the second landing, her arms crossed over her chest and a smug grin on her face. She sticks her leg out to halt Dannie's progress.

"What?" Dannie asks.

"When did you meet a boooy?" Alex singsongs the last word.

Dannie's throat grows dry. Boys don't just come visiting her unannounced. She kicks Alex's foot aside.

"Hey, hey, hey, little sister," Alex says. "Just be yourself. Well, maybe be a little *less* yourself and a little more me because I'm obviously your coolest sibling."

"Not helping, Alex."

Alex laughs but lets her past. Dannie races down the rest of the stairs. Sam, Jo, and Charley are all in the entrance hall.

Damn. There's *really* no privacy in this house. How did she ever think living with four older sisters would be any sort of good idea? Fine.

The main door is open, but the glass one isn't. Horace stands on the porch with his back to her, looking out at the leaf-covered front yard.

Taking a deep, steadying breath, she opens the glass door. "Heyyy, Horace. W-what are you doing here?"

He turns. He's wearing dark, well-fitting jeans and a black hoodie over a green plaid shirt, with his knit beanie and full beard and . . . Holy shit, he's hot. And she is awkward. So, so awkward. Being a vampire was supposed to save her from sweating too much and getting her tongue all twisted when she tries to talk, all the sort of stuff that happens to hormonal teenage girls.

"Dannie! Hey."

She almost swoons at his smile. What a pathetic excuse for a predator she is. "Hey, hi," she says and immediately cringes. Normal people greet others once. Freaks greet them three times.

"I haven't seen you," says Horace. "How's the night shift treating you?"

Her fangs pop out. They're still new enough that it sends an ache through her upper jaw. Holy shit. Is this normal? Is this a normal thing that happens? That is a completely legitimate and necessary thing to warn your little sister about! They may be older (well, not technically) and more experienced and, frankly, scarier, but she's gonna make them pay.

Stay cool. Be Alex. Be *any* of her sisters. "You know, no complaints."

"Cool."

She chuckles nervously, bringing a hand up to her mouth to hide her fangs. "Yeah. Totes cool."

Behind her, her sisters snigger. She compresses her lips. Idiot, idiot, idiot. She better come to terms with her awkwardness because immortality is a long-ass time.

"So, I haven't seen you since your birthday party," he says. "That was a lot of fun, by the way. Liked the gothic theme. Very cool, good for October."

"Thanks. It was my sisters' idea. My whole family's into that stuff."

"I've noticed. Oh, speaking of . . ." He turns around to pick up two potted plants at his feet and presents them with a flourish. "Here. It's, uh, a blood orchid and a blood lily. Sort of a late birthday gift."

She accepts them with a broad smile. "Blood flowers? How . . . unique."

The color drains from his face and his heartbeat quickens, niggling at the hunger in her veins. She should've fed on her way home from work this morning.

"I was wrong, wasn't I? Man, I'm so stupid. I just thought with the party and the new aversion to day shift and how gorgeously Amazonian your sisters are, and how your parents still look like they're in their twenties . . . Scott told me I was delusional. Now you probably think so, too. Oh, shit, I'm so sorry."

"Wait. You think my sisters are gorgeous?"

Laughter from the entranceway. Awesome. As if this weren't embarrassing enough. Her rule is never to date guys who have seen her sisters first. It creates false expectations.

"Well," he says, "in the sort of way that you can recognize that your crush's family has great genes. Respectfully, that is."

"Right," she says. He's nervous and adorable, and if he really knows and is okay with it, maybe the whole vampire-human obstacle is one they can get around.

Wait. Crush?!

"So, you're not terrified of my family? You're not scared off by—" *Bloodlust and undeadness and the possibility of having all the blood sucked straight out of your veins?* "By what we are?"

"You mean an intelligent, loving family, every member of which can beat me at arm wrestling?" He cocks his head. "Or do you mean vampires?"

She sighs. He said it. That means she can acknowledge it, right?

"Yes, that one," she says. "I mean us being vampires."

"Oh, good." He raises clenched fists in a restrained gesture of victory. "Everything added up in my mind, but, I mean, I didn't want to show up at your front door with actual blood because that's pretty weird no matter how you slice it and there was the matter of where I would even obtain such a thing, but also, like, what if I'd been totally wrong and just came off looking like a giant freak?"

She lifts an eyebrow. She's gotten really good at intimidation brows since last week.

"But the answer is," he says, "they're really not so bad. I think after they get to know me, they'll even like me. And 'scary' is definitely not the adjective I would use for you."

"No?" She clears her throat.

Someone nudges her, probably Sam because then Sam whispers, "Ask him what adjective he *would* use, you dolt."

"Oh, dear Lord, she's useless," says Jo. "How did we go so wrong?"

Vampirism should come with a handbook, like how to flirt with a real, live boy and how to rid herself of annoying siblings. Horace scratches the back of his neck. Autumn suits him. His scent is all cinnamon and cloves and musky man. He's life in the midst of decay, the promise of rebirth.

Too bad her social ineptitude has sparked warnings from her brain. *Abort. Abort mission. Abort conversation. Abort crush, move away, change your name so he can't find you.*

Dannie snaps herself out of it. "Well, uh, you probably need to get to the library. Boss'll kill you if you're late. Thanks again for the plants. They're lovely."

"Right, work," he says with a nod. "Can't be responsible for students not finishing their papers on agency and Victorian governesses. And you're welcome. Guess I'll see you around."

"Okay. See you around."

He turns and walks down the porch steps, taking his beautiful face and his beautiful beard with him. Shit, shit, shit.

"Someone's got to save this," Alex says. She leans into the doorway and shouts, "What adjective *would* you use to describe me?"

Their voices are similar enough, and Alex has withdrawn from sight by the time Horace spins around.

"That's the thing," he says, "I can't pick just one. Or—" He strokes his beard, considering. "—if I were going to, I guess it would be 'indescribable.'"

Vampires do *not* get butterflies. That's ridiculous and most definitely not what is happening to her right now. "That's . . ."

Sweet. Endearing. Romantic. Perfect. Any of those would suffice.

"Ask him out," comes Charley's fierce whisper from behind her.

"Actually," Horace says, taking a step forward, "the reason I really came here was to ask you something."

Dannie tilts her head. "Sure. Anything."

"Would you, uh, would you mind if I switched to night shift, too?"

She can't help the ludicrous grin on her face. "No. No, I wouldn't mind that at all."

"Great."

"Great."

"See you at work, then."

Another nudge between her shoulder blades. She clears her throat. "Or, you know, outside of work."

"Outside of work?"

"Yeah, for drinks maybe. Saturday night before my shift."

"I'd love that," Horace says. He lifts his hand in a wave and retreats down the path to the sidewalk.

Yes, yes, yes. Her stomach *clearly* thinks she's still in tenth grade because it's doing these nonstop nauseating flip-flops, but that's not important right now. What's important is that a man exists who, despite knowing her true nature, doesn't see her as scary or weird or anything like that.

It's not until he's around the corner that she steps back inside, closes the door, and leans against it. His smile warms her so much that she can almost ignore the four women swarming her.

Charley takes her arm. "What kind of a name is Horace? He wasn't born in the nineteenth century. Or was he? Should we look into his background?"

"Am I the only one who's concerned that he's human?" Sam asks. "Mom and Dad are gonna flip their shit when they find out."

"Ah, come on," Jo says with a dismissive wave. "She's allowed to experiment. We should be thankful she's got a date at all."

"And he's smokin'. That helps," Alex says. She flings an arm around Dannie's shoulder and says in a low voice, "Nerds in love. It's so cute my heart just might start beating again."

Dannie, unable to quit smiling, gently pushes her sisters away. She may not be as graceful or as stunning or as dynamic as they are, but maybe she doesn't need to be. Maybe she only needs to be comfortable in her own skin, even if that means she sometimes thinks like a human and can't win at any family games and still likes terrible music.

"You are all horrible, and I love you," Dannie says as she jogs up the staircase, "but now, if you don't mind, I'm going to bed. Try to entertain yourselves without me." She runs her tongue over her fangs.

You know, maybe her life doesn't suck so bad after all.

Steeping Spells

Here's the thing about mortals, Ainsley muses, leaning her hip against the tea counter. They rarely know what they need, and when they do, they can never figure out how to get it.

Jill, one of SinceriTea's regulars, has been staring at the menu for six minutes even though she always orders a chilled green tea. Always.

Finally, Bianca at the register asks, "Your usual?"

Jill fidgets with the hem of her sleeve. "Sure."

"You doing okay?" Ainsley asks, setting to work on the drink.

Jill groans. "I have a big presentation tomorrow. Going to be up all night." She lifts her arms to show sweat stains on her white button-down. "I'm sweating to death already."

See, this is the sort of thing that makes Ainsley grateful she's not a mortal, bogged down by silly mortal things. She wasn't made for jumping through ridiculous hoops. Doesn't mean she can't feel bad when someone else has to. She turns her back to Bianca and adds a dash of creativity and another of focus, small sparks of pink and green jumping from her fingertips.

She waits for Bianca to give Jill her change before handing over the to-go cup. "Well, I'm sure you'll kick some corporate ass, and be sure to drink that up."

Jill smiles. "Why do you think I stopped here? Your tea always makes me feel better."

"Appreciate that, Jill. Break a leg."

Jill's barely out the door, sending the bell jingling, when Bianca crosses her arms and raises an eyebrow. "I saw that."

"Saw what?" Ainsley asks, refilling one of the samovars.

Bianca leans forward. "You know, someone's bound to figure it out sooner or later."

"Please. The human mind can rationalize the most bizarre happenings."

"Ainsley," Bianca says. The unspoken argument in her eyes is one she can't say aloud—that the city is cracking down on unregistered magic users, Ainsley among them.

But Ainsley has always been a little too stubborn for her own good, which is not a fantastic rebuttal.

Two things happen at once, and one of them annoys Ainsley much more than the other. A patron in the corner drops their mug of tea, which crashes to the floor and breaks, and Detective Evelyn Tempest walks in.

Otherwise known as the bane of Ainsley's existence.

"Speak of the devil," she mutters.

The detective is a tall woman, taller than Ainsley, which is irksome. She wears her normal outfit of an open suit jacket, a maroon button-down shirt tucked into dark jeans, and sturdy boots on her feet. Aviators cover half her face, and her brown hair's pulled into a ponytail, so tight Ainsley's surprised she doesn't have a constant headache.

Bianca veers off to take care of the spilled tea and broken mug while Ainsley takes up a veritable battle position behind the counter, grumbling all the while.

"Can I help you, Detective?" she asks as Tempest approaches.

Tempest lifts her sunglasses and perches them on her head. "Miss Devereux. Always a pleasure."

"For you, maybe," Ainsley says sweetly. Before the other woman can respond, she asks, "What can I do you for, Detective?"

"Right." Tempest flicks her gaze over the menu above their heads. "Do you have any night owl tea? I think it's a relatively new blend."

An unusual request. Not many people even know about it, given that it's infused with magic.

SinceriTea *does* carry it, but it's not on the menu, and it's not a tea she gives out to detectives. Not without an excellent reason.

Ainsley, gearing up for the bickering that always accompanies the detective's presence, crosses her arms. "Doesn't ring a bell."

"Really?" Tempest raises an infuriating eyebrow. "I find that hard to believe."

So, it's going to be one of *those* days.

Tempest puts her hands on her hips, jacket open to expose her gun and badge. A power move? Seriously?

"This isn't an interrogation room, Detective, and I'm not a suspect. At least as far as I know."

"You're going to make this hard on me, aren't you?" Tempest says, leaning over the counter and dropping her voice, "Ainsley, I know about the magic. I know about *you*. Have for a long time. So, cut the bullpucky already, all right?"

Ainsley gives a long-suffering sigh she saves especially for the detective. "Why do you want to know?"

"Because that's our agreement. You give me info on the magical black market, and I turn a blind eye to the fact that you're selling magical goods without a license."

Oh, come on. She *barely* sells magical goods. A few splashes of good vibes here and there, some tea that has a little extra kick. Nothing big. But Ainsley decides to let that go with a huff. "No, I meant, why do you need to know about night owl?"

Tempest grins, that grin she gets when she thinks the case she's landed will interest Ainsley. Well. Looks like today isn't going to go quite as planned.

"First, tell me if you sell it," Tempest says.

"First, tell me your order," Ainsley retorts.

"You're impossible. Why do I even work with you?" But Tempest is already digging in her pocket for her wallet.

"You don't work with me. Because *someone* is too prickly for a partner, even one not from the precinct." Ainsley says it with a touch of warmth, though, because they both know Tempest's history with partners. They never last very long. Some of them hate the magical aspect of the job and transfer to a different department. Most are just scared of her.

"You're a pain on the best of days, Miss Devereux."

"You can call me Ainsley, you know."

"Earl grey hot chocolate to go, please."

The amount of times Ainsley rolls her eyes in the detective's presence is astounding. Maybe she'll go for the world record one day. She takes the payment and sets about making the drink.

"Now will you tell me if you sell it?" Tempest asks, leaning on the counter, looking cool but very much like a cop. "The night owl?"

"Yeah, I sell it, but not very often."

"Who typically buys it?"

Ainsley hands over the to-go cup. "College kids, mostly. They mainline it during midterms and finals. Sometimes newish moms. People working late. Anyone who needs an energy boost and needs to get stuff done."

Tempest sips the tea, makes one of those 'ah' noises people make when a drink's too hot.

"Don't burn yourself," Ainsley says, her voice too dry to be taken as legitimate concern. She's chomping at the bit to know just what the detective has up her sleeve, but she won't let Tempest know that.

"We've had some weird reports lately, all having to do with water."

"Water?"

"Mm-hmm. A lot of daytime swimming in fountains. A lot of late-night swimming in the rivers. That sort of thing. We've had to put extra security on the rivers."

A chuckle escapes Ainsley's lips. "Seriously?"

"The only thing every case has in common is that the perps are tea-drinkers and they live within a few blocks of here."

Ainsley furrows her brow. If she sold a hallucinogenic substance without knowing it . . . Well, let's just say Petey has a lot to answer for.

Tempest pulls out her phone, shows the screen to Ainsley, and plays a video. "Recognize this guy?"

Onscreen, a gentleman strips down to his tighty-whities and splashes into the fountain over by the stadium, scaring away geese in the process. A police officer on a bicycle stops and approaches the man, who's waving his arms and shouting.

"What's he saying?" Ainsley asks.

"He claimed he was a merman and that was his domain." Tempest tucks the phone back in her jacket pocket. "You didn't recognize him?"

Ainsley shakes her head. "I'm not out at the counter all the time. Maybe Bianca or someone else does."

Tempest nods. "I'll ask in a minute. First, I'd like to take a look at the night owl you have in storage."

Ainsley groans. "You're asking a lot, Detective."

"Actually, I think if you take a deep breath, you'll find I'm being quite reasonable."

"Fine. But can I finally get a badge or something? A nametag?"

"No."

Rolling her eyes again, Ainsley motions for Bianca to take over the register and leads the detective back into the tiny stockroom, its shelves packed with boxes. She takes down their only box of night owl and takes it through to the breakroom, where there's an electric kettle. She brews tea all day. She doesn't want to wait for her own to steep.

Tempest paws through the box at the table while Ainsley starts the kettle.

"That won't help," she says. "The magic's in the steeping."

"Is that so?" Tempest asks, but she lifts her hands from the box.

Ainsley, arms crossed and resting a hip on the counter, considers the detective and the predicament that's accompanied her. Whatever's in the tea can't be *that* harmful, can it? "Anyone gotten hurt yet?"

"Not yet."

Good. That's good.

"They don't really seem to be interested in harming themselves or anyone else. They just really like water."

Good and kind of funny.

When the kettle finishes heating, Ainsley scoops some night owl blend into the infuser, sets the infuser in a mug, and pours the steaming water over it.

Tempest comes to stand beside her. "How do we tell if it's regular night owl or—"

"Something else?" Ainsley murmurs. "Well, we drink it."

"Be serious, Miss Devereux."

"Call me Ainsley, and maybe I'll consider it."

"The quicker we figure this out, the quicker I get out of your hair."

"Or is it the other way around, Detective?"

Tempest lets out a little huff. "Can you just do the spell now, please?"

"Sure, sure." Aside from the little sparks she injects into tea, Ainsley hasn't done a spell like this in a while. Magic isn't meant to be used frivolously. She takes a deep breath, wraps her hands around the ceramic mug, and whispers a revealing spell.

The tea morphs from golden-brown into glaring neon yellow.

"Well, shut the front door," Ainsley mutters. "We need to talk to Petey."

"Who's Petey?"

"Petey!" Ainsley shouts as she grabs the doorknob of his townhouse without bothering to knock.

Tempest puts a hand on Ainsley's arm. "Whoa, whoa, whoa! We have to do this properly. We can't go in without probable cause."

"But he always leaves it open. He's an idiot."

"We can still knock first."

"Fine," Ainsley grumbles, but she pounds on the door and yells his name again. After a brief pause with no answer, she makes an exaggerated gesture at the door. "See?"

Tempest knocks—more politely—and calls out, "City Police. Is there a Peter Kelley at this residence? I'd like to speak with him."

Still no sound from inside.

"Probably in the basement," Ainsley says. She cups her ear and holds a finger to her lips. "Do you hear that, Detective? Someone's . . . I think someone's calling for help." She barges into the townhouse.

"Miss Devereux!"

Ainsley heads down the basement steps, Tempest on her heels. Sure enough, Petey's on the couch in ripped jeans and a beanie, playing video games, a few empty bottles of beer beside him.

He's a clurichaun, which means he's either playing pranks or getting drunk. She's been the butt of a lot of his pranks, but they're generally stupid and harmless and always directed at her, not her customers. Fake snakes in boxes of inventory. Harmless stuff.

"Ainsley," Petey says without taking his eyes off his spaceship-racing game. He does a double-take when he sees the detective. Then he shoots to his feet without pausing the game and salutes. "Officer."

"Relax, Petey," Ainsley says. "She's a friend."

"Oh. Um . . ." He offers an awkward bow. "Would you like a refreshment?"

"No, thank you," Tempest says, perfectly at ease somehow as she introduces herself and shakes Petey's hand.

Ainsley plops into an overstuffed armchair. "Petey's my middle man."

"Ah, yes," Petey says with a fond smile. "The water folk are crafty creatures. Ains isn't such a fan."

Not anymore, at least.

Tempest perches on the edge of the ottoman. "So, you procured Miss Devereux the night owl tea?"

Eyes narrowed, Petey looks at Ainsley. "If you're looking for a refund, I'm afraid—"

"Listen," Ainsley says, leaning forward with her elbows on her knees. "People who have been drinking the night owl tea from my shop have been displaying unusual interest in bodies of water. That's obviously not the intended side effect of night owl, so I need to know if you laced the batch."

"Of course not. I don't touch the goods."

Ainsley glares.

"Okay, I *mostly* don't touch the goods. But I didn't touch the night owl. You're the only one of my customers who even orders the stuff." He crosses his arms, looking like a petulant child. Which he kind of still is. "Are you happy now?"

"Do you know who else could've tampered with the order and whether they would've done it intentionally?" Tempest asks, voice patient.

"I don't know." Petey shrugs. "Anyone who touched it before I got it, I guess. I don't ask questions about where my stuff comes from."

Tempest hums. Then she asks, "Who's your supplier, Petey?"

Petey looks right at Ainsley. "You're not going to like it."

Tempest escorts Ainsley out of Petey's house and then makes her wait while she takes a call from the precinct. Typical.

Ainsley leans against Tempest's car, a black sedan that screams "cop." She really doesn't mind the detective. Tagging along on cases can be kind of fun, and bickering with Tempest is even more fun.

Tempest pockets her phone and says, "The city lab analyzed the tea. They didn't come up with anything."

"I could've told you that," Ainsley says. "Magic isn't exactly detectable."

"And magic isn't exactly permissible when prosecuting. This is why you can't be my partner."

"Hey!"

"And now, I have to go actually be a cop," Tempest says. "I trust you can make it back to SinceriTea on your own."

"Sure," Ainsley says. She can. Not that she's going to. When Tempest unlocks her car, Ainsley aims for the passenger's side.

"What are you doing?" Tempest asks over the top of the car.

Ainsley pauses, already gripping the handle. "Coming with you."

Tempest's lips twitch. Then she jabs a finger at Ainsley. "You're staying in the car."

Ainsley counts it as a win. "Here's the thing about magic, Detective," she says as she slips into the passenger's seat because she can't resist. "It's not dangerous. It's not something to fear. It's something to be taken care of, something to be nurtured."

Tempest gives a dismissive little grunt and pulls away from the curb. "Your point, Miss Devereux?"

"Magic is everywhere. You just need to open your eyes and let it in." Ainsley waves a hand between them. "Like this partnership. Magic."

Tempest taps her fingers on the steering wheel. "We're not partners."

"Whatever you say, Detective. Whatever you say."

Cities have arteries, veins, a heart at its center, just like any being—mortal or otherwise—walking its streets. In this city, it's quite literally in the water. The rivers are the lifeblood of this place, both in the mortal world and the magical one, and the docks are where the two intersect.

Considering the docks represent the life she left behind, Ainsley hates them. Or, at least, she tries to. Even after so long away, there's something about the fresh scent of the river in her nostrils and the sight of the stacked shipping containers that sets her at ease. Just for a moment.

She follows Tempest, who hasn't asked why Ainsley's so off. She probably won't, either, because she's just that polite. Annoying.

As they approach the main warehouse, Ginny Greenteeth emerges. She doesn't literally have green teeth, thank goodness, but her hair, cropped short, has a tinge to it reminiscent of algae. She's a stocky, powerful woman in more ways than one. She used to scare the daylights out of the neighborhood kids by pretending to curse them. Never scared Ainsley, though.

"Well, well, well," Ginny says. "If it isn't little Ainsley Devereux. To what do I owe this honor?"

"Ginny," Ainsley says, inclining her head.

"I doubt you're here to bury the hatchet."

Tempest looks between them curiously, but still, she doesn't say a thing.

Ainsley stuffs her hands into her jacket pockets and balls them into fists. "It was a long time ago, Ginny."

"Not long enough, I guess. You brought a cop?" Ginny says, voice gruff from cigars and whiskey.

Tempest holds up her badge. "Detective Evelyn Tempest. I just have a few questions, Ms. . . ."

"Greenteeth," Ginny says.

"Well, Ms. Greenteeth, We don't mean any trouble. We just want to get this sorted out and be on our way. It seems at least one box of night owl tea you sold to Peter Kelley has, um . . ."

"It's infused with the wrong spell," Ainsley says. "It's supposed to be help people focus and get their work done faster, but it's just been making people think they're mermaids or something."

Ginny doubles over in laughter. Tempest raises an eyebrow at Ainsley, who offers a shrug in answer.

When Ginny finally comes up for air, she wipes her eyes. "That explains so much. You see, the selkie crew that lives in the river give their kids a special tea that helps them commune with the water." She turns to Tempest. "They can't live full-time in the water until after puberty, so the spelled tea encourages them, the shy ones especially."

"Oh, right," Tempest murmurs like it's not new information.

"Maisy must've gotten the spells mixed up between the batches. The lass has always been a little spacey."

"That's it? This was all just a big mix-up?" Ainsley asks. How anticlimactic.

"'Fraid so, darling," Ginny says. "Don't worry. We'll get you a new box. No charge. Petey'll bring it around in the morning. And it won't happen again. You have my word."

"I'll be sure to test it before I sell it this time," Ainsley says.

"Wouldn't expect otherwise."

"Thank you for your time, Miss Greenteeth," Tempest says calmly. She holds out a business card and offers her hand. "Feel free to call me if you ever need anything."

"Sure thing, Detective. You take care now."

It's a clear dismissal, and Tempest disappears among the shipping containers.

When Ainsley follows, though, Ginny says, "Lot of people 'round here wouldn't mind seeing you, Ainsley. You remember that."

It's not an order, just a reminder. Ainsley appreciates that. With her back turned, she pauses, nods once, and heads to the car.

Ainsley finishes wiping down the last table just as the bell above the door tinkles. "We're closing," she says without looking up.

"According to my watch, not for another nine minutes," says Detective Tempest.

Ainsley rolls her eyes. "Such a stickler for the rules." Except when it comes to whatever this little agreement is. She's pretty sure the chief doesn't exactly approve of their unofficial partnership. And that's totally what it is—a partnership.

"Someone's got to be," Tempest says, somehow shrugging and stuffing her hands in her pockets at the same time.

Ainsley saunters back behind the counter. She tosses down the rag, flips on the kettle, and leans on her elbows. "Is that why you're here? To fine me for not having a license?"

Eyebrows raised, Tempest looks around the empty tea shop. "What's this? You don't have a license?" Then she laughs. Evelyn Tempest, the woman who never seems to even crack a smile, laughs.

Gasping, Ainsley clutches her heart. "I'm sorry. Does the precinct know Detective Tempest has been body-snatched?"

"Okay. Okay. Just get me a tea, would you?"

"Coming right up." Any day Detective Tempest comes a-calling promises to be an interesting one. She's even starting to enjoy their collaborations. A little bit. "Do you think there's a spell out there that can make me think I'm a fire spirit? That'd be cool."

Tempest snorts. "Like you need any more fire, Ainsley."

Ainsley pauses as she grabs two to-go cups. She smiles. Then she fills the cups with boiling water and lets Tempest have her pick of the teabags.

Tempest picks an earl grey. Of course.

Before Ainsley hands over the cup, though, she subtly adds a white spark of tranquility. Seems like the detective can use that at the end of a work day, no matter how big or small or silly the case.

Ainsley chooses a bag of dragon well tea.

"I, uh . . ." Tempest clears her throat, flips out the tail of her jacket, and settles at the tea bar. "I think I have another case that might benefit from your expertise."

Ainsley sits on the stool behind the counter, dipping the teabag in and out of her cup. She grins at the idea of tackling another case, this time unrelated to her own establishment. Hopefully. "So, we're partners now?"

"No," Tempest says. "Absolutely not."

"Nah, we solved that case because of *my* contacts. I think that makes us partners."

"I would hardly call that a case. It was an unfortunate error."

"Not to the people who thought they were mermaids. Or selkies, I guess." Ainsley plucks the tea bag from her mug. "Say it. We're partners. Unofficially, of course."

Tempest squints into her tea. "Unofficially. Let's start with that. I think the next case can wait till the morning, though."

At least Ainsley has something to look forward to tomorrow.

They sip in silence for a few minutes until it's officially closing time. Ainsley accompanies the detective outside and takes her time locking the door.

"Thursday nights are poker nights," she says.

"Excuse me?" Tempest stands on the sidewalk, one hand on her hips, coat open and Aviators on. She's such a cop. It's almost insufferable.

"My friends and I do poker nights. Gary's hosting tonight's. He usually has a good beer selection."

"Oh, that sounds fun."

"Do you want to come?" Before the surprise can register, Ainsley adds, "I should prepare you. It's not your usual crowd."

Tempest lifts her eyebrows in a silent question. *Magic folk?*

Ainsley nods.

"I suspected as much. The outlaw type, too?"

Ainsley thinks of her hodgepodge group of friends—witches, of course, but also a fae, a couple shifters, even a ghost. "The law-adjacent type, more like."

"I think I can live with that."

"Good. Just . . . be less cop-like."

"What does that even mean?"

Ainsley gestures up and down at Tempest's outfit. "You know. Don't be so you."

"I don't understand. I'm me. How can I be less me?"

Ainsley rolls her eyes, but not for the first time in this bizarre friendship, the gesture is a fond one. "Come on, Detective. I'm feeling lucky tonight."

"Are you?" Tempest drawls. "Because your shop still needs a license."

Ainsley throws up her arms. "You cannot seriously hold that over my head all the time."

"The solution is simple. Just get the license."

"It's expensive. Besides, I don't sell that many magical goods anyway."

"Mm."

"Wait. Isn't your aunt the mayor? Can she get me a discount since you won't?"

At the End of the World

Parker walks.

She's been walking for days through forests growing greener with each hour, as if, in the absence of the majority of humanity, nature has remembered how to breathe, how to nurture itself. Good for her.

Good for Parker, too. The shifts in terrain get her heartbeat up, tire her out faster. And her canteen has been empty for a day. It shouldn't be long now.

It's going to suck.

When she can no longer bear the tremble in her legs, she lies down in a clearing dappled with sunlight. Slowly, torturously, the surrounding cacophony resolves into recognizable sounds. She picks out warblers, chickadees, wrens before her knowledge runs out.

It's nice to hear nature come back to herself, reclaim her space, her time. She spent so long on the defensive. She and Parker have that in common, then. The difference is that Parker is tired, the kind of tired that leadens her bones and makes it feel like she's sinking even while she's on solid ground.

The difference is Parker let it break her.

Parker wakes.

Her heart seizes within her chest even as her lungs fill with air. She's not supposed to be breathing. Her heart's not supposed to be pumping blood through her veins like the world is normal, like the body it's keeping alive wants to be here. She was supposed to die back there in that field, and now . . . Now she's alive, lying on a cot in a strange room with white cinderblock walls, an IV tube stuck in the crook of one arm. The fluids it administered must have brought her back from the brink.

Damn it.

She's stripped down to her tank top, and her dirty flannel lies folded on a plastic chair under the window. Her boots sit beneath the chair, socks tucked inside. Her jeans are still on, though, which is somewhat reassuring. At least whoever grabbed her was more interested in keeping her alive than in harming her.

There's only one problem with that.

She rips the tube out.

The concrete floor is cold on her feet before she slips into her socks and boots. It doesn't matter where she is or who's brought her here. All that matters is that she gets out and finishes what she started. Her stomach churns at the prospect of dehydrating and starving herself. This next attempt is going to be even worse than the first.

She grits her jaw. She's broken, yes, but she's not so broken that all her resolve has slipped through the spaces between the shards. Only most of it.

She pulls on her flannel shirt, buttons the middle, and opens the door to a hallway with walls as hard and blank as the ones in the room.

And a woman.

"Whoa, whoa, whoa," the woman says gently, hands up to intercept Parker. Her jeans are dusty and torn at the knees, and she wears a ratty t-shirt under a loose vest. "Slow down, there. You should be resting."

"No, I shouldn't," Parker says vehemently. She swivels on her heel and heads in the opposite direction, no clear destination in her mind except out. She has to get out so the vise around her stomach and lungs will ease.

"All right. You want to take a walk? We can walk."

If the other woman isn't going to leave her alone, Parker might as well get information out of her. "Where am I? How'd I get here?"

"Or we can walk and talk. That's good, too."

Her smile is kind, but Parker's stomach is clenching and unclenching with a fierce desire to run. She stumbles down the hallway, illuminated by sunlight coming through the windows.

"We were out on a supply run when I found you. Your canteen was empty, so I got some water down your throat, and we put you in the back of the truck. Nothing to it, really."

Parker snorts. Like this woman just goes around rescuing every stray she finds.

"Probably lucky I found you when I did, actually. Another few hours . . ."

Yeah, well, she didn't ask for that.

"As for the where, this is a refuge of sorts," the woman continues. "It's a walled compound that used to belong to a cult. Still some of their weird pictures and stuff around. Anyway, we found it a couple years back. Decided to stay."

Parker keeps walking, taking a right at the next intersection. Why is this woman talking so much? Can't she see that Parker doesn't care, that Parker would rather be dead than be listening to her chatter?

"Everyone's excited you're here, me included. We don't get new people very often. One more to fill the beds and work the fields."

Parker pauses at an intersection.

"Left," the woman says.

"What?"

The woman raises an eyebrow. "To go outside. I assume that's what you're after."

Parker goes left.

The other woman stays on her heels. "I'm Lucy, by the way." She says it matter-of-factly, as if finding a stranger close to death and bringing her to her used-to-be-a-cult-compound home and then finding out she doesn't want to be there is an everyday occurrence.

Finally—finally—Parker reaches a door with an 'Exit' sign overhead and punches the touch-bar. She races down the four or five steps but stops when she hits grass.

She hunches over, hands on her knees.

In.

Out.

In.

Out.

She's still alive—unfortunate—but she's out of that concrete maze. She'd thought nothing could be worse than empty, endless forest, but at least she could breathe there.

"Hey, hey, hey," the woman—Lucy—says. "Why don't you sit down? I'll get some water."

"No. No, I'm fine."

"Are you sure? You're pretty pale." Lucy puts her hands on her hips, drawing away the sides of her vest. The movement reveals a gun at her side. It gleams in the sunlight.

The aim forms immediately even if the plan doesn't. No matter what, Parker's going to get her hands on that gun. She straightens. "Lucy."

Smiling, Lucy nods.

For the first time, Parker looks at Lucy with interest. She looks into startlingly green eyes, the eyes of the woman who will be indirectly responsible for her death. "Parker. My name is Parker."

Parker follows.

From what she can tell, the compound is expansive. The buildings stretch on in all four directions, and Lucy tells her the property is sixteen square acres, all encompassed by a reinforced steel fence. The building they've come from is the infirmary, although she'd been deposited in a separate, less furnished room as they assessed her condition and made sure she wasn't a threat to the others. The housing district takes up the compound's eastern block, which is presumably where she'll stay.

Or where they want her to stay.

"This is the mess," Lucy announces as the gravel path they're on meets another hideous square of cinderblock.

Wow. These cult people really didn't have much of a sense of aesthetic. Not that it would've saved them. If nothing else, though, prettier buildings could've made the collapse of society a little easier to bear.

"Hungry for dinner?" Lucy asks. "I'm starving."

At the head of the line, she hands Parker a tray like it's the most exciting thing in the world. Like Parker just moved to town and it's their first day of senior year and Lucy drew the short straw to show her around. Like this is anything close to normal.

The line shifts incrementally. The food seems decent. At least it's fresh and cooked, two things she couldn't always achieve on her own.

"How are you happy all the time?" Parker asks.

Lucy takes a brown roll from an overflowing bowl. "What do you mean?"

"You're always smiling, but there's nothing left to smile about, not anymore. Nothing even to live for."

Lucy is quiet as they move down the line. Parker fills her plate with fresh greens and vegetables, a yellow apple, mashed potatoes, and a slab of venison. A decent last meal.

Then Lucy says thoughtfully, "There was a time I thought that, too. But after a few months, I realized the things that made me smile back then still make me smile. Moonlight rippling across the grass, excruciating puns, poetry."

Parker stares disbelievingly until the person behind her huffs impatiently. Uneasily, she picks up a glass of orange juice. She'd thought that kind of optimism had died with most of the population.

"What about you?" Lucy asks kindly, leading the way to a table occupied by three others. "What made you smile in the old world?"

As they approach, one of the three people, the one with stubbly hair and a scar on her upper lip, says, "You're lucky, Queen, getting out of duties to watch over the invalid."

Ignoring the jab, Lucy sits and introduces her friends.

Jane Riddick, the one who'd spoken. She's big and burly, and black tattoos poke out from beneath her t-shirt.

Liam Blake, with cool blue eyes and a boyish grin.

Sydney Spencer, whose wire-rimmed glasses are held together in the middle with electrical tape.

Parker sits beside Lucy. Her leg jiggles relentlessly. She doesn't have to remember their names or make nice with them. She has to stay here only as long as it takes for her to get her hand on Lucy's gun. To give herself something else to focus on, she digs into the venison, which is tough but better than anything she's eaten in months.

"They're just jealous," Lucy says. "We all have chores we're expected to get done, but I was doing my assigned work."

"As long as we get 'em done," Blake says, "we can do whatever we want to in our free time."

Can they not tell Parker doesn't care? About this place, about how it works, about these people, about this kind of non-life?

"Except leave the compound," Riddick says.

"Right."

Parker points her fork at Lucy. "You did."

"That was a sanctioned run," Spencer explains. "Only people who leave are the patrol."

Blake elbows Lucy teasingly. "Sawyer—"

"She's the patrol leader," Lucy says to Parker in an undertone.

"—hasn't let any of us in yet besides Lucy. She was the first of us to pass fight training."

"Fight training?" Parker asks around a mouthful of mashed potatoes. This place is sounding more and more like a boot camp than a refuge. But maybe that's what humanity needed to survive the end of the world—old-fashioned military force. Gonna beat Mother Nature into submission. She suppresses a laugh and instead asks, "Just fists? Or do you learn with weapons, too?"

Blake puffs up a bit and says, "I've moved on to knives."

"They let you polish them. Don't make it out like you're some bigshot," Riddick says, snorting. To Parker, she says, "The patrol gets guns, though. Even more exciting."

"Yeah," Lucy says, "that's why they haven't let any of you knuckleheads in yet." Her tone's teasing, and her smile's soft. She's an odd duck. She fits in—she's even a leader of sorts, at least among this crew—and yet she doesn't.

Riddick slams her palms on the table. "Well, kids, it's been fun, but someone drew dishwashing duty tonight. Nice to meet you, Parker. Welcome to Campocalypse." She snickers as she walks away, tray in hand.

A minute later, Blake and Spencer walk out together, and Parker notices Lucy's finished eating, too. She shovels mashed potatoes into her mouth a bit faster.

"Take your time," Lucy says, chuckling.

Parker slows down.

"I'm done with my duties for the day, and you won't get any until the doctors check you out tomorrow and pronounce you fit for work." Lucy shrugs. "It's just free time before curfew at ten."

"I don't have to sleep on that cot again, do I?" Parker asks.

Lucy rolls her eyes. "Tom and Jaxon dropped you there before I could tell them to put you somewhere comfier. Sorry. They're not the smartest."

"But inside? I'll be sleeping inside?" Parker has to ask through a strange lump in her throat.

"Most solo arrivals stay in the hospital until we can get housing sorted. We don't like people staying alone. But, uh . . ." Lucy clears her throat. "A couple of us sleep out in tents in the center field. You could share mine."

Parker nods. It doesn't matter whose tent it is if she doesn't have to sleep inside four walls.

She grabs the apple and takes a bite. "How do you usually spend your evenings?" She doesn't care, not really, but it's polite to ask.

Lucy's eyes sparkle. "Come with me."

Ten minutes later, following a brisk walk in the deepening twilight, they're on the other side of the campus.

Parker expects to have to feign her reaction, but her jaw drops in surprise when Lucy opens an unassuming door and lights a handful of lanterns inside. Shelves cover the walls, and books cover the shelves. There must be thousands. Parker hasn't seen this many books in one place since before the end. She breathes in deeply, inhaling that heady, musty scent that takes her back to a different life, when people who loved her moved through the rooms of a creaky wooden house and the world hadn't gone to the dogs.

Somewhere behind her, admiration tinging her voice, Lucy says, "Nothing but a hundred copies of their version of a holy book when we showed up. I try to get at least a few books every time I go on a supply run."

The books are even organized by genre. Probably Lucy's doing. That seems like something she'd care about. Parker picks up a copy of Mary Shelley's *The Last Men* and flips through, unleashing even more mustiness. The yellowed pages are marked up in pencil. Whoever had owned this once had loved it well. Or maybe just used it for a college paper.

"You can keep it," Lucy says.

Parker turns.

"Well, not keep it, but take it out. Like a real library. Can you believe it?"

Believe that this place has attempted to restore order to an orderless world? Sure. Believe that they've actually succeeded, at least in mass meals and organized books and some semblance of harmony? No, not really. Maybe there really is some good left in the world.

Maybe.

Lucy crosses the room, plucks a book from a shelf, and flops into a leather armchair. "Well?"

she says, that strange smile on her face again. "What are you waiting for? Gonna stay awhile?"

Parker stares.

A lantern sits in the center of the tent, but the canvas ceiling is coated in shadow. She fingers the corner of the cover of *The Last Men*. She's clean, freshly showered for the first time in years, and Lucy's found her an extra sweater for the chilly night. By all accounts, she should feel wonderful.

But she's not the sort of person who feels much anymore.

Outside the tent, whispered voices.

"She's practically feral," says one. Riddick, maybe?

"Shut up." That voice belongs to Lucy. "She's seen shit, just like everyone else who ends up here from the outside," she says, voice pitched low, but not low enough. Scuffling, then, "Get out of here. I don't have time for this right now."

Shortly after, Lucy ducks into the tent, a sheepish smile on her face even in the low light. She settles into a sleeping bag. "Sorry if I snore."

"I don't mind," Parker says. Her nights—and days—have been so silent that it'll be nice to hear any sound made by a fellow human. Not that she's planning on doing much sleeping.

After shucking her boots, placing them at the head of her sleeping bag, and setting the gun inside one, Lucy blows out the lantern. Darkness falls.

Parker continues to stare at the ceiling. Not too long now. She licks her lips. This is the opportunity she's been waiting for, so why does her heart feel like it's going to explode?

"What happened?" Lucy asks.

It's so soft Parker isn't sure if she heard it or not. Could've been the wind. If anyone left on Earth could understand, maybe it's the girl who doesn't quite fit in here no matter how hard she tries.

Before Parker can consciously refuse, the words are tumbling out. "When the end came," she says, voice husky, like she's in the midst of the smoke again, "my family and I found a camp of survivors. We stayed. I mean, what other option was there? Try to survive on our own?"

Maybe that would've been the better option. They could've lasted longer. Or they could've gone together. Either way, she wouldn't be alone right now.

Lucy waits for her to continue. Already, Parker can tell she's patient as a saint, kind as one, too. After all, Lucy's the type of person who believes there's still something worth living for.

This isn't living, though. This is just surviving.

"After a year, it almost started to feel like we were safe." Like the disasters wouldn't come again to wipe out more of the world, more of humanity. "But that wasn't true." She rolls onto her side, back toward Lucy. "That's never true, is it?"

Parker waits.

Lucy's soft snores fill the tent. After Parker had shut down the conversation, Lucy hadn't taken long to fall asleep. Everything about this is routine for her—right down to the crazy girl she's taken under her wing.

Not for Parker. Nothing is routine about the last night of your life. She inhales and exhales deeply until her heart stops pounding quite so fast. But she can't put this off any longer. She can't endure this any longer.

She sits up and takes off the borrowed sweater. No sense bloodying it when the next new arrival could use it. Hands trembling, she folds it and sets it aside. Then she laces up her boots.

Even after sitting in the dark for an hour or more, her eyes haven't adjusted. Still, she can judge where Lucy's head lies and, just above that, her boots with the gun tucked inside. She slides her hand over until it connects with a boot and then up until she feels cold, hard metal. Her fingers curl around the handle.

It's heavier than she expected.

Outside the tent, the air is cooler, and she fills her lungs. One of the last tastes she'll ever get.

It's sweet.

She tightens her grip.

Where should she do it? No matter where, she's going to wake people up, so maybe she should at least go into the woods. Minimize the amount of people who'll be traumatized by her corpse.

Lucy stumbles out of the tent.

Parker whirls.

"What the hell?" In one heavy heartbeat, Lucy's eyes go from bleary to shocked. Then she lunges.

Her weight throws Parker off balance. The landing knocks the breath out of her, but she's with it enough to hold the gun away from Lucy.

"I'm not going to let you do this, Parker," Lucy says. She clasps Parker's wrist and bends it backward.

"Stop!" Parker gasps as soon as her breath comes back. Pain radiates through her wrist. "I need this!" It comes out as more of a growl than a shout.

She *is* feral. These people are better off without her. Lucy is better off without her.

Something hard connects with her skull.

The world goes black.

Parker sits.

They've locked her in the same white room as before and let her stew through the night. Through the window set high into the wall, she's watched the fluctuations in light from the setting of the moon and the rising of the sun. It must be midmorning by now. If she's waiting, she's not sure what for. Are they going to execute her? Is that what weird, motley groups who are insane enough to live in a cult compound do at the end of the world? Or would exile be a more likely outcome?

Her head throbs. She fidgets with the gauze bandage around her temple to keep her focus off the pain.

The door creaks. Lucy appears, her mouth twisted with uncertainty. She approaches slowly and then chooses to lean on the windowsill.

A few moments pass. Parker concentrates on the steady rhythm of her heart. *Ba-doom. Ba-doom. Ba-doom.* It keeps time until her fate is revealed.

"The others think you're a danger to the group," Lucy says. Her arms are folded, and her gaze rests on the tips of her boots, like she's disappointed.

But that doesn't make sense. To be disappointed in a person requires that you trust them, believe in them. No one could believe in Parker.

In the midst of those thoughts, she finds her voice. "And what do *you* think?"

"I think you're a danger to yourself, not anyone else." Lucy's shoulders heave as she sighs. "Look, I know from the outside, the world looks pretty awful. Every morning, we get up, and we have to fight until we make it to the end of the day only to go to sleep wondering if we'll live to the end of the next day. Life is hard now, harsh. But it was hard and harsh before, only in different ways."

Despite her ache to stop living, to stop breathing right now, Parker asks, "So, what keeps you going? What keeps you from going crazy and wanting to blow your brains out like I seem to want to do every second of every day?"

Lucy contemplates. "The fireflies have come out again. That time of the year, I guess. And if you go to the eastern block, on the second floor of that yellow house with the red shutters, there's a broken window that lets you out onto the roof. Sometimes when I'm not on duty, I watch the sunset and stay to watch the stars. That's pretty nice. And the library's full of books." She chuckles. "For the first time in my life, I actually think I'll have time to read everything I want to read."

Parker stares.

"It's the little things, I guess, the immeasurable things." Lucy says it like she's telling herself, not Parker.

Like she's pleading for Parker to choose to stay.

"Why do you care about me so much?" Parker asks. "Most of the world is dead. Why would one more body matter?"

Lucy shrugs with one shoulder, gaze still focused on the floor. "Feels like it matters. Feels like everyone matters now. You asked me what there was to live for now. But what was there ever? The world was terrible, and our country was a big contributor. I wanted to be a lawyer, but I couldn't afford to go to college. Even with scholarships, the loans would've buried me before I could pass the bar."

Parker closes her eyes. Since that day, all she's wanted was to go back to how it was before. If her life had been harder, would she be harder, better equipped to deal with the world as it is now? Would she be as strong as Lucy?

"You know what I was doing the day society died?" Lucy says. "Working three part-time jobs, at least two shifts every day, no days off, and that was barely keeping my head above water. I hated my life, hated what I had to put up with in order to survive. But I loved my family, my friends, too. We lived for love, and what do we live for now? The same thing. But, hell, I'm not going to force you to keep breathing if all you want to do is stop."

Parker's stomach feels like lead. It weighs her down, pins her to the cot. Lucy's disappointment hurts worse than her head.

"So, yeah, maybe you're right," Lucy says. Her voice is strained, hoarse with something Parker can't name. "Maybe nothing matters anymore." She pushes off the windowsill.

Tears burn hot in Parker's eyes. She fights them, but she doesn't fight the shame that takes root in her chest cavity. She's been on her own for so long, mourning the people she's loved and lost, that she didn't recognize this place for what it could be—a second chance. And she's been so hell-bent on joining them that it blinded her to the possibilities of what Lucy was offering. Not perfection, not returning to her old life, but healing.

Is that enough? Could it ever be enough?

On her way out, Lucy pauses with one hand on the doorknob, slides her gun from its holster, and sets it on the table between the door and the bed. She doesn't look at Parker when she says, "Wait until dark. There's a cemetery on the west side of the compound. Beyond that, the forest starts. No one will hear you from there, and it'll be close enough to the cemetery that I can bury you tonight. I can give you that, at least."

Then she's gone and the door is closed, but no locking click comes.

Lucy's given her what she's wanted. Only the prospect turns sour in her mouth.

Parker trudges.

Lucy must have told whatever authorities exist in Campocalypse that she's not a danger to anyone because they let her go without a fuss. They let her walk toward the edge of the compound property, one fist clutching a gun.

It gets heavier as she goes. Her entire body feels heavy, her bones turning to stone. As she approaches the woods, she stops. She tilts her face toward the sky, letting the sun warm her skin.

In.

Lucy had believed in her, believed she could make a go of life here.

Out.

If her family could see this place, they'd believe that, too. They'd want her to live.

In.

But what does *she* want?

Out.

Her life here wouldn't be the same as her life back then, her life with her family.

In.

But it would be living, and living is way more than just surviving, way more than what she's been doing for endless days now.

Out.

That might be enough. She could try to make it enough. It's not perfect, but it might be an adequate place to start.

She sits down, sets the gun beside her. The grass is soft beneath her butt, and she places her palms down, too, to feel the softness on her skin. Her baby sister used to say she felt more at peace within nature than she did anywhere else. Even after nature had turned on them, she found that peace in little moments, moments small enough to bundle up and drop in her pocket to save for a rainy day.

Kind of like Lucy.

The grass prickles Parker's neck and arms as she lies down. Closing her eyes against the sun, she reaches for the peace her sister used to talk about, reaches for something other than the emptiness that's been following her around since they left her alone. By the time she opens her eyes once more, her heartrate has slowed and her body feels light, as though she's a plant turning the sunlight into energy, transforming it into a will to live.

Above, the sky goes from blue to gold to orange to red. Even as it darkens to purple and finally to black, even as the stars appear, she doesn't move.

She doesn't move until the first firefly makes itself known.

In the apple orchard, where she finds Lucy, Parker lets go of the gun. It slides into Lucy's palm, and with it goes everything Parker's been clinging to since her family died and she survived.

Shock.

Pain.

Anger.

Overwhelming, crushing sadness.

She hasn't shed them for good, but she's done with letting them control her. She's in charge of her life now.

Lucy doesn't say a word, simply holsters the gun and looks expectantly at Parker.

"Engineering," Parker says softly. "I liked building things."

"Well." Lucy's eyes are full of relief and something like admiration. Like she's proud of Parker or something equally crazy. "We could definitely use an engineer's brain around here. And someone's got to keep Charlie from implementing all his bad ideas."

Nodding, Parker swallows that lump in her throat that had bubbled up again. She feels the words for what they are—a peace offering, a promise that she doesn't have to talk about it unless she wants to.

"Come on," Lucy says. "We've got work to do."

Parker smiles, a thin thing that doesn't quite touch her eyes but holds the promise of healing.

Lucy smiles back, and when she beckons this time, Parker follows.

The Bleeding Heart

The pirate boy is late. He's often late, though, often distracted by the island's vibrant flora or finding himself entangled in new adventures. But as surely as *The Sea Wolf* is docked, he'll be here. He promised. Isaiah doesn't break promises.

Miranda settles where the water meets the rocks. Black scales shimmer as she moves her tail languidly to keep herself in place. The color is rare, her black tail the only one between the Spanish colonies and the English. She's careful, though, keeps away from ships and most humans.

All but one, really.

The cove, shining in silver, is secluded enough for a private rendezvous but exposed enough to let in the starlight. The surface is different than life underwater. Below, silence encompasses you. Above, the moonlight, open air, and salty sea collide. It feels free, the air filling up her lungs, but confined, too, like the sky is crammed with possibilities.

Life itself is crammed with possibilities—now that she's charted a course. In a little while, less than a day, nothing will stand between them, not even the boundless and unshakable ocean. Her nerves flutter. It's scary, giving up everything you know, trading sea for sky—blue for blue, vastness for vastness. It won't be that much different. And she'll have Isaiah.

That is all that matters.

Miranda calls out to him.

My love, where are you?

Her people believe when you fall in love, truly in love, you can communicate without words. Miranda had thought it only a legend. How surprised—and delighted—they'd been the first time Isaiah had heard Miranda's thoughts.

Her parents refuse to believe it. They say a human cannot love a mermaid. They say humans will want her only for the value they create in their own minds.

No. They're stuck in the old ways, stuck in a time when they had this world to themselves. She can't afford to listen to them.

"I'm sorry! I'm sorry!" the pirate boy calls, still out of sight.

Yes, Isaiah is all that matters.

He appears around a jumble of rocks and dashes across the sand, one hand clutching his tricorn hat, knee-length coat flapping in the wind.

He reaches the water and throws himself to his knees on the rock. "I'm late. I'm sorry."

"You're always late," Miranda says, plucking the hat from Isaiah's head and perching it on her own, "and you're always sorry. You are getting to be predictable."

Isaiah gasps. "You take that back! I am no such thing."

Miranda laughs. She's constantly surprised by the lightness in the sound above the surface, or perhaps the difference is Isaiah's doing. "I will not. Now, what tales have you for me tonight?"

Grinning, Isaiah lies on his stomach so they're at eye level. He shines. Golden hair shines even without the sun, his lips are full and magnificent, and his eyes are a vibrant blue like the waters surrounding them. He is nature itself—sand in his hair, ocean in his eyes, earth under his nails, fire in his heart. He is in love with life, and Miranda is in love with him.

The first time Miranda saw the pirate boy, she thought she'd lost her way and happened upon an island inhabited by gods. Isaiah was born to be viewed from underwater, dazzling and murky. Miranda will never see him like that again, but she'll also never forget how hot the sun had been that day or how green the foliage or how perfect the moment.

"We spotted *The Siren's Wail* two nights past," Isaiah says.

"The ship you pirates say is crewed by ghosts?" Miranda toys with a tassel hanging from Isaiah's coat. "And what did you do? Were you brave? Did you fearlessly lead your men into battle?"

"There was no battle. And they're not my men."

"Not yet. Someday. Someday soon."

Distracted by the lap of the water, Isaiah overlooks the reassurance. In the softness of moonlight, untempered by the waves, his handsomeness is more entrancing. Will Miranda grow accustomed to that? Will her breath come easier when that day comes?

Isaiah frowns, causing a crease to appear in his forehead. "Besides, how do you combat ghosts?"

He is young—older than Miranda by a summer but oh so young. Humans are incorrigible, stubborn creatures. They want to figure things out for themselves, make their own mistakes rather than rely on the wisdom of countless generations.

"You don't combat ghosts," Miranda says. "You let them be. There are things that aren't meant to be disturbed in this universe, and ghosts are one of them. Ancient, cruel, not bound by the rules of the world." She shivers at the weight of her own words.

"The rules of the world," Isaiah scoffs. "Why should *we* be bound by them?"

He takes Miranda's hand, and Miranda's heart skips at the contact. Isaiah's skin is rough, callused over hers, but his touch is warm and affectionate.

"Even captains must bend to the rules of the world," Miranda says, "and so must you, too, if you want to be one."

Isaiah, sighing, flips onto his back, but he keeps their hands locked, his arm pulled across his body. "There's unrest among the crew. Robinson . . . He's a madman. He'll drive *The Sea Wolf* to the bottom of the ocean in this quest for revenge."

Robinson the Red, so named for the blood on his hands. Miranda and her people stay out of sight of that ship. The story above goes that he lost his wife to a sea monster and is bent on tearing out the creature's guts with his own hands. Below the surface, the truth is not that simple. It's known that the monster had not devoured his wife but instead that the cursed animal *is* his wife. The obsession is understandable, then, but no less terrifying.

"Well, if that happens, you'd at least be with me," Miranda teases. She runs her thumb in circles over Isaiah's skin. "Isn't that what we've always wanted?"

Isaiah's breath hitches.

It won't always be this way. They'll have each other and the sand between their toes—her toes—and when Isaiah is away, Miranda will keep their cottage tidy and make mosaics from the storm glass. And keep vigil. She does that now anyway.

Miranda sobers. "Robinson bothers you so much?"

"There's unrest, talk of upheaval," Isaiah says. "Only we need someone who can counter him."

"You can counter him. You deserve to be captain over a madman."

"I'm not sure the men will follow me—not unless I can prove myself."

Miranda reaches up to wrap her arms around Isaiah's shoulders. Water rolls from her skin onto his coat and shirt. She brushes her lips over his ears. "Then show your strength. It shouldn't be difficult. You're the strongest person I know."

Isaiah starts. He hooks his hands onto Miranda's arms. His voice, so robust and commanding, becomes quiet. "I'm not. I'm weak."

"Weak for me?" Miranda hums.

"Mm, since the moment I saw you."

"That might be because I saved your life."

Miranda may have noticed the pirate boy, but the pirate boy hadn't noticed her, not until Miranda pulled him from the ocean following a storm. The waves had broken *The Bleeding Heart* into firewood, and many of the crew had been lost at sea. Miranda and her people make it a rule not to interfere with humankind, but she had been powerless at the sight of the waves dragging down the pirate boy.

"When that storm came," Isaiah says, brushing his thumbs over Miranda's arms, "when I fell into the sea, I knew I was dead. I knew the ocean would take me for its own. But I woke. I woke after thinking I would never feel the sun again, and instead an angel was bending over me. My angel of the waters."

The sea laps at Miranda's waist. This is nice, holding him beneath the stars. This calm, easy love will be the rest of their lives.

"I owe you my life. I owe you so much," Isaiah murmurs.

"You owe me nothing beyond what you wish to give to me."

"I don't want to talk about this anymore," says Isaiah. "I want to talk about the secrets the stars are hiding. I want to talk about the whispers in the wind. I want to talk about you. Tell me what adventures you've conquered in my absence."

Miranda laughs. "Life in my world is not as it is on land, you know."

"I know," Isaiah says through a sigh. He sits up and turns around, takes Miranda's hands in his own again. He's tactile like that, needs to stay connected. "It's quiet, peaceful."

"You would hate it."

"But I would love you. That might be enough."

"Of course it would be. For such a smart boy, you sometimes have very little sense."

So nonsensical, so ambitious, so strong. Her pirate boy.

It's a dance they do, pretending each can live in the other's world. Only now it's possible. The news thumps against Miranda's ribcage like it will burst right out of her chest. She can conceal it no longer. "There is something—something important—I need to tell you."

"Yes?"

Placing her arms on Isaiah's knees and leaning up, Miranda whispers, "I know how to do it. I know how to trade my tail for legs. And for longer than a night, too."

Isaiah's cheeks whiten. "You mean your immortality. You'd be trading your immortality."

"And what of it? What is immortality to me without you to share it with?"

All the riches in the sea wouldn't be worth an endless life without love. She'll miss home and her family, certainly, but they can arrange to see each other every once in a while. Everything else will hardly be a sacrifice at all, not in the face of blinding affection.

"You will forget about me," Isaiah breathes. "In the span of eternity, I am a grain of sand, nothing to concern yourself over. You shouldn't have even noticed me."

"How could I not notice you?" Their meeting was fate, their love written in the stars. "No more talk of this. Let us speak of other things."

Isaiah glances down at their entwined hands. He looks sad, but who could be sad on a night that holds such promise? "We may speak of other things, but you will still intend to go through with it. When? Tomorrow?"

"Do you want me to wait?" Miranda lifts a hand to Isaiah's cheek to turn his face toward her. "Will you please look at me? I want to do this. I want to do this for you. So we can be together."

Everyone—her parents, the privateers, the islanders—laugh at them. They say love cannot last. But they are wrong. The best kind, the purest, lasts, and this is the best kind.

The cove is tranquil, and the night air is cool against her skin. The stars protect them above, the water below. A pleasant fuzziness builds in Miranda's chest. It's as though the universe itself has blessed them.

Isaiah takes a lock of Miranda's curly black hair between her fingers, exposing the dark skin of one breast. His voice carries an undercurrent of sadness when he asks, "What are you thinking about?"

Miranda smiles and brushes her lips over Isaiah's fingers.

You are the buzzing in my brain, she says. *You are the thrum of my heart, the rush of blood through my veins. You are the sea that enfolds me in its arms. You are the sand that clings to my skin for fear of releasing me. You are the stars that shine behind my eyes. You are the marrow in my bones and the hope in my heart.*

Isaiah's lips quiver. He hates crying, but he's close now.

Aloud, Miranda says, "I am thinking about how radiant you are and thanking whatever god is responsible for your form and your light."

"Don't say that," pleads Isaiah. "Please don't say that, any of it."

"Why should I not? It's true."

Isaiah rests his forehead against Miranda's. "Because I do not deserve you and never shall," he says, breath ghosting over Miranda's lips.

Miranda's eyes slip shut, and she loses herself in the closeness. Hardly any space remains between them. But Isaiah's breathing is ragged, his hands trembling.

"Kiss me," Isaiah whispers. "Please?"

Isaiah never asks. He always takes.

Isaiah offers a shaky smile. "A mermaid's kiss is lucky."

It's easier to overlook in the moonlight, and Miranda, unable to stop herself, surges forward to press a kiss to Isaiah's lips. He tastes of salt—like the sea, like Miranda's home. He tastes of truth.

That familiar tingle in her lips is followed by numbness. It creeps through her mouth and down her throat. A heaviness settles inside her chest, spreads to her limbs so that they feel leaden.

Isaiah slides his arms beneath Miranda's and props her up.

Miranda opens her mouth—or tries to. No words escape.

What is happening?

Isaiah's face crumples. "I'm sorry. I'm so, so sorry."

Realization sparks in Miranda's brain. *What have you done? What have you* done?

"I coated my lips with a paralytic," Isaiah says, his eyes shining. "You know your worth. You know how rare you are. If I bring you back, the men will listen. They will elect me captain."

I would have given up eternity for you, and you have sold me in the name of ambition. This isn't strength. This is weakness.

The hat topples off Miranda's head as Isaiah pulls her onto the rock. It bobs on the water before being taken by the waves and disappearing into the blackness.

"Yes, but I warned you," Isaiah says. "I have always warned you."

And Miranda was too foolish to heed it.

We could have had what we wanted, the only thing we ever wanted. Her lips are heavy, and her words are slurred even in her mind, but she soldiers on. Isaiah needs to hear these things.

Miranda wants to plead. She wants to tell her they could still have what they want. Isaiah can take it back, and she will forgive him, and they can live.

But "I need you" is what Isaiah says. His voice has lost all its strength. "I need you so I can be captain."

That cottage, that life, will never be. Isaiah would first need to want to be forgiven, and the pirate boy is much too proud for that. He has made his decision.

Miranda burns to say it. She forces the words through her lungs and up her throat and into her mouth, and still they will not come.

For this, you will burn in hell, but first you will live through it.

Isaiah binds Miranda's wrists, no longer harboring the strength to look into her eyes.

Above them, the stars blaze.

Isaiah was wrong. Miranda will never forget the pirate boy who bled her heart dry.

Uneasy Lies the Head

Purple clouds obscured the moon, but torches lighted the courtyard below. She stood at the windows of her chambers, looking down at the servants as they erected a scaffold in the center. The pounding of the hammers reverberated straight through her bones. Goosebumps rose on her arms. She rubbed them away. With a sigh, she adjusted her crown.

"You could spare him."

She turned. A lanky young man stood by the hearth, the shadows accentuating his height. The hemp rope around his wrist marked his status as an indentured servant. His name was Pate.

She smoothed the folds of her velvet gown, a deep blue that reminded her of the sea at night. "I don't believe it's any of your concern." She reached for the flask of wine on her desk.

Never taking his eyes from her, he strode across the chamber, took it from her hand, and filled her goblet. He handed it to her with a smile.

No. Pace. That was it. His rich brown hair gleamed in the firelight, and he had slender yet strong hands equally skilled in reverence and passion.

Or so she imagined.

He returned to the hearth and knelt to add another log to the fire. Spring carried such a chill in the air, and the stones of the castle seeped up the cold. She sometimes thought this room could never be warm again.

"He's your brother," he said, face still turned away.

The wine tasted of cloves. Images flashed in her mind—a blond boy running through sunlit fields, arms outstretched to catch the violets racing by. How innocent she once was, how trusting.

She sank into the wooden chair, placed her hands on the carved lion armrests. "A brother who attempted to dethrone me."

She returned to the parchment spread across her desk—maps, lists, figures. She was drowning in numbers, in facts, and wanted only a compassionate hand to pull her from the quagmire.

She sipped her wine, swirling the piquant liquid around her tongue.

That hand did not belong to her brother.

She closed her eyes and pressed the heels of her palms against them. When she opened them once more, though, the ink still blurred under her gaze. She really should go to sleep, but she couldn't recall what it felt like to lie down without the paralyzing fear of what lurked in the shadows.

Pace returned to stoking the fire. An able-bodied young man like he was didn't belong in domestic service, but she'd gone through so many servants lately. They'd fled in waves to her brother's camp, lured by the promise of higher wages, fairer working conditions, and healthier crops. It was a better life they wanted, but they couldn't see she could give it to them just as well. She needed only time. A dying kingdom couldn't be revived in a day, and even with her brother's defeat, the servants hadn't yet returned.

"Still," Pace said, "you must care for him."

Without looking up, she made a correction to a sum on one chart amid dozens. "Why do you say that? Because we're blood? I think he's proven that means very little to him."

Though her brother was younger by a year, she looked up to him, sought his approval. He'd had a smile that made her feel she could fly and a knack for making her laugh.

How many months had it been since she saw that smile? Years?

An ink stain blossomed on her forefinger. She bent her head to her papers once more. The top sheet reported the state of her troops. She read it for the twelfth time in an hour and slid it beneath the pile. Even as she concentrated on the numbers, reports, and maps before her, Pace hovered by the hearth, well within her periphery.

She set down her quill and looked up at him with calculated coolness. "Yes?"

He fiddled with his plain bracelet. She wondered if it encumbered his mind as well as his wrist.

"It's only . . ." he began. "Have you eaten supper tonight? A queen who works through the night without nourishment is not fit for her duties."

"Not fit?"

She raised a brow at him, but he smiled as though she were a silly peasant girl to indulge rather than his sovereign to serve.

"I only meant you must take care of yourself," he said.

Had she eaten? She couldn't recall much of this night, save for numbers that blurred together and a burning knot between her shoulders.

And the muffled *thwack, thwack, thwack* of hammers from the courtyard.

Why did he care? Being kind while doing his duties would not break his indenture any sooner. Servants weren't kind; they were obedient. Most were content to accomplish their chores without so much as a glance her way, and some even went out of their way to avoid meeting her unexpectedly in the corridors, to avoid the muted hush of these chambers, to avoid her.

She studied him for a hint of a motive. His tunic hung on his angular frame, and he'd had to cut an extra hole in his belt to fasten it around his trim waist. His was the classic body of a peasant who knew nothing of what it meant to be properly fed. What could kindness mean to a man like that?

A boy, really, for that's what he was, clean-shaven still.

She nodded. He executed a neat bow and strode from the room. She stared at the empty doorway. Then she shook her head, cleared her throat, and studied the chart in front of her. What made him think she couldn't decide for herself whether she was hungry? Yet when he returned, the aroma of roasted capon and potatoes drifted through the room and made her stomach rumble.

He set the tray in front of her and poured a fresh goblet of wine. He handed it to her, a crooked smile on his face, and she pretended not to notice his fingers brushing hers. She could not disregard, however, his brazen closeness as he walked around to her side of the desk and began clearing the papers from it. Or the faint scent of smoke and sweat.

"I didn't ask you to do that," she said.

He shuffled the papers into a stack and set them on the windowsill. "No."

"Then bring them back. I'm not finished."

He tapped the supper tray. "Eat first. Then work."

She sipped the wine, and her lips tightened in a frown. "How bold you are. But how very unbecoming boldness is in servants."

Chuckling, he turned away, took the bed warmer, and filled it.

"Tell me," she said, watching the curve of his shoulders as he placed the warmer in the hearth. "How did such a man come to be in my service?"

He straightened, the fire throwing shadows on his face. "The typical way, I suppose," he said softly. "My parents died, left me in debt, and I was told there was work to be had in the castle."

"No one's great ambition is to be a domestic. How did you have the misfortune to be stuck in such a position?"

"I volunteered. I heard stories of the lonely queen in her tower, sitting up at her desk all through the night, a single candle burning."

She ate a forkful of potatoes.

"I wanted to see for myself if they were true and, if so, why a queen should be so . . . solitary."

She cleared her throat. "And what have you found?"

With a tilt of his head, he said, "I find it's an honor to serve you, my queen."

She took a bite of capon and swallowed before saying, "There's more work, better work, to be had outside the castle. Were you not tempted to join the usurper?"

"Is that what you call him, truly?" He put his hands on his hips, which only accentuated the narrowness of his waist.

She swirled the wine in her goblet, watched the red liquid go 'round in the silver cup. "'Brother' seems not to suit any longer."

"It might again someday."

She looked up sharply.

He said, "Mercy must temper judgment, surely."

She leaned back in her chair. "Too much mercy opens the door for betrayal."

"Too little," he said, "blinds you to the true loyalty you do possess."

"What would you know of loyalty?"

"I know one mustn't forsake it."

She tapped her fingers against the lion heads. "Loyalty forsakes a person, not the other way around. I look, and all I see are faithless people. They long for change they don't want to wait for, don't want to work for. And he . . . he used that to his advantage."

She took a long swig of wine as he stood silent for a long moment. A fuzzy warmth suffused her, though she couldn't say whether from the fire across the room or the goblet in her hand.

Then, "If that is what you believe . . . then perhaps you are not the queen this country needs."

He turned the bed warmer over in the fire to heat the other side, as if they spoke of the weather and not the misgivings which crept into her heart in the darkness of night, weighing on it until fissures formed. How long until the cracks drove through completely?

She tilted her head and narrowed her eyes at him. A candle was not the only means of repelling the dark.

"Why are you here?" she asked. "Truly."

"Even a queen needs someone to confide in, does she not?" He took a hesitant step toward her. "Perhaps she may even need counsel at times."

Supper sat forgotten.

Far from reminding him of the boundaries which separated and yet bound them, the rope around his wrist seemed to erase them.

"What would you counsel, sir?" Though she'd meant to be mocking, the words came out broken and drained.

"Forgive him. Free him. Break with him. Offer peace."

Peasants thought in such simplistic ways.

"As co-regents, you could bring this kingdom back to life," he pressed.

"Why," she asked, "does a servant care who sits on the throne as long as his family doesn't starve?"

He gazed at her with eyes that were more gray than blue. She saw intelligence there, a fire he held back only with great control.

"Because I believe," he said, "together, you could rule this kingdom with benevolence and mercy, restore it to its former glory. Some things cannot exist without their opposite. How could we value sunlight without the dark? You and your brother cannot be completely whole without the other. Your mother knew this, I think."

She ran a thumb over the florets carved into the silver goblet. "What know you of my mother?"

"I know her sigil depicts sun on one side and moon on the other. Like you and your brother, neither can exist without the other. And I know she'd not like this quarrel of yours."

Her thumb paused over a raised blossom. Her blood turned to ice, and, despite the fire he'd built up, all warmth drained from the room.

At the time of his capture, her mother's sigil had been in the possession of her brother. He had kept it on his person, so close that she imagined he didn't freely discuss it. Now, she had it with her at all times, away from servants' eyes.

Her voice was foreign to herself as she asked, "How did you know about that?"

He paled but made no reply.

She stood. In a low yet emphatic voice, she asked again. "How did you know?"

"I've heard reports," he said even as he dropped his gaze to the floor. "That's all."

"Reports," she repeated with a scoff. "Is he your master?"

Pace dropped to a knee. "You are my queen, and I would have no other."

"I would have you join him in the dungeons tonight and on the scaffold tomorrow."

"Cruelty is no virtue, my lady."

She took his chin in her hand and wrenched his head upward to look at her. "I am your queen, and you will address me as such."

"Yes, Your Grace."

She pushed his face away. "Weakness is no virtue, either."

The gray in his eyes had nearly overtaken the blue. Calmly, he asked, "Is that truly what you think? That this is strength? Then I pity you. May you one day know the mercy that you refuse to show."

"May you find consolation in your master's defeat by going with him to the grave."

He stared at her, his gaze piercing, and opened his mouth. How would he plead for his life? Would he plead for it at all? There was a tiny part of her that would consider pardoning him if he did.

But he said nothing.

"Guards!" she called, and he dropped his head.

The autumn sun beat down upon the courtyard, and a bead of sweat ran down her temple as she stood on the platform. Her crown weighed on her head.

Three men stood over trapdoors, their hands tied behind their backs and nooses around their necks. The man she once called brother was in the middle, his head hanging and his blond hair gleaming in the sunlight. The man on the left was his right hand, an oversized warrior whose strength proved useless now.

And the last . . .

She inhaled sharply and looked away. She nodded at the royal executioner, a burly man who stood on the opposite end of the platform, dressed in a heavy black cloak.

"You are accused of high treason," he began in a loud, clear voice, "for the act of conspiring to overthrow the rightful queen. For this, your penalty is death. Do you have any final words?"

The prisoner on the left spat in her direction.

The man in the middle lifted his head and looked at her. Voice husky, he said, "Nothing good comes from blood against blood. We should have known better, you and I. My wisdom came too late. I would that yours does not."

A dull ache spread through her heart, and she wished for a goblet of wine to chase it away. She lifted a hand.

"Wait."

The last had spoken. The executioner looked to her for confirmation. The prisoner's gray-blue eyes paralyzed her.

"I've not yet spoken," he said, his words strangled with emotion. "I forgive you, though I wish to the heavens I could have helped you."

Her fingers trembled in the air.

She dropped her hand.

The trapdoors fell.

The Real Lizard Wives
of Earth

"June! June!"

Jiusyndor continues down the street. She's on a mission. She has to get to the pet store to pick up their largest bag of flies and one of crickets (if she buys too many at one time, the silly people in polo shirts get suspicious and start asking how many snakes she has and if perhaps she'd be interested in a larger cage for them?). After that, it's off to the hardware store for some industrial-sized bug zappers before picking up Bilamaggron from soccer practice.

Which is why it takes her a moment to remember she's June. On this world, at any rate. A good, safe Earth name. Boring, if you ask her. One she can barely trouble herself to remember.

"June!"

She plasters on a smile to the fleshy face that still feels so . . . mushy, and she turns around. A group of Earth women descends upon her.

"We thought that was you!"

"I'm the same way! Always off in my own little world!"

"Yes, so many things to be thinking of! The whole day needs to be planned, and we're always thinking of the next step! Isn't that right, ladies?"

Of all the things she hates about this planet, what she hates the most is the women. In no particular order, they are self-absorbed, jealous, petty, and . . . 'Bitchy' is the term for it. She'll never get used to it. Even with the silly parent-teacher organization at the middle school, there are so many trivial disagreements. June thought she'd left that all behind. If she has to mediate between the mothers who want to sell candles as a fundraiser and the mothers who want to sell chocolate one more time, she's likely to shed her human disguise and give them all a piece of her decidedly non-human mind.

Still, these women have children in Billy's class. It pays to be polite. Or, hopefully, it will pay. One day.

"Hello," she says sweetly. "I'm just on my way to the pet store."

"Oh, yes, I heard you let Billy keep a snake," says one of the women. Carl, maybe. Or wait . . . Carol. That's right. Carol shudders. "Nasty creatures, aren't they?"

June straightens. She hasn't actually seen a snake—not in person. On this thing they call the YouTube, though, yes. "I happen to think they're lovely, intriguing creatures."

"Right, but don't you have to feed them mice? Live mice?" asks another, Gail. She's chubby and really quite scrumptious, but she always wears clothes that are too big and hide her form. Like she's ashamed of it. Can you imagine?

"Oh, leave her alone, girls," says Pam.

That's another thing June will never understand—why women insist on referring to themselves in the juvenile form. It's like they have no respect for themselves as mature beings. Then again, Earth does seem to prize youth and beauty above all.

Oh, not above money. So: money, youth, and beauty.

"Anyway," Deb says. She seems to be the leader of the clique. "We're on our way to happy hour at Galaxy's. Thought you might want to join us."

Cars pass in whooshes. The shouts of children spill from a park down the block. A bell jangles as the door to a shop is opened. The walk signal at the nearest intersection begins to beep. The women stare eagerly at her.

Oh. Right. They're waiting for her to speak. That was . . . an invitation? Earthlings are so informal. Honestly.

"Oh," she says. "Oh, no. I don't think so. I'm really quite busy tonight."

"A rain check, then?" asks one. Sharon?

A rain . . . check. She understands those words separately, but not together. In the interests of getting away (and getting those delectable treats to Mowsondran so he can make dinner), she nods. "Of course. A rain check."

"You should go," Billy says from the middle seat of the minivan.

June flicks her gaze toward the rearview mirror. Her son is covered in mud from soccer practice. When winter comes, they'll all be praising Rotharnogak for a little process called homeothermy. Why ever did they settle in the American northeast? This is where they crash-landed, sure, but this planet is advanced enough for long-distance travel.

"Mom!" Billy says, louder this time. "I said you should go."

"What? Go where?"

"To the bah-runch thingy."

June frowns. "It's 'brunch,' and how do you know about that?" Telepathy doesn't usually appear until puberty. If it's manifesting early, they'll have to have a long talk about how humans don't like when you know what they're thinking without them saying it. They're primitive that way.

He bounces the ball on his muddy knee. "The other kids' moms were talking about it at practice. They said they always invite you but that you never go. I think you should go."

"And why do you think I should go?"
"You need friends."
June blows through the stop sign.

The first invitation she accepts is one to book club. It's a bit more formal than the others—in an email—and so June feels more comfortable than with their usual, casual invitations. The book of the month is one about a circus that only opens at night and has magical tents. June enjoyed it, but her one critique is that all the characters were human.

So, with Billy's encouragement in her mind (and a reminder to play nice), she totes the copy she bought last week into Carol's house.

"Welcome!" Carol says, leaning in to the kiss the air just in front of June's cheeks (another custom she'll never understand. Why not just kiss the actual cheek? Humans didn't seem to be afraid of each other's skin too much). "Come in! How do you like the house?"

It's large, but June knows enough that that's not a thing you say even if the owner of the house wants everyone to know their house is large. It's a far cry from her own decorating tastes, though, so she says, "It's very . . . white!"

Carol beams. She seems to take that as meaning it's very clean. "Thank you! Let me get you some wine!" Carol probably liked the book because there were so many white tents in it.

As she's led into the kitchen, also white, she wonders if these women ever speak with periods instead of exclamation marks. The wine (also white!) is tasty, though. She has two glasses before she even gets into the living room, where she settles at the edge of the sofa with the book on her lap.

And—and here's something she didn't expect because who would have ever expected it?—the women don't seem to have actually read the book. Their copies—library copies, of course—sit untouched on the coffee table. Their wine glasses, however, don't. Their wine glasses leave their hands only for refills.

After her third, June finds she doesn't mind. The smile on her face won't seem to go away, and she's learning so much about Earth culture. So much! She knows that Beyoncé is queen, that *Mulan* is the best Disney movie, that there are fifty shades of the color gray (Why Earthlings need so many is a question for another day. Not that there will be another day, of course).

These women, though. (*All* women, really!) For all the months she's been on this planet, June has had the exact wrong impression of its women. They're not self-absorbed; they focus on themselves every once in a while to preserve their sanity because they're asked to do everything and get no thanks for it. They're not jealous; they've been taught only so many women can succeed and so they have unlearning to do when they're adults. They're not petty; they've been given purview over such insignificant matters that they're forced to make them significant.

And they're certainly not bitchy. In fact, June is starting to think that's a word males (human males) came up with to keep women who live outside the lines down.

"Will we see you next week?" Deb asks, and she looks so hopeful June can't say no. She simply can't. It would be like pulling off a young one's tail only to teach them a lesson before they realize it'll just grow back in a few days. That's cruel, and June's not cruel.

June is also very interested in drinking more of this wine. So she waves and smiles and says, "See you next week!"

On the drive home, she tells herself it's only research. On the dominant species of her new planet. Yes, research.

"Why didn't I like you ladies for a long time?" June asks over the thumping music. "You're so much fun!"

It's ladies night at Galaxy's (the starry swirls on the ceiling are not accurate at all, but they are quite entrancing), which means they get half-priced cocktails, and they are going all out. June thought she'd hate it, thought she'd spend the night sulking and making excuses to get away as quickly as she could, but there's music (Earth music is so upbeat!) and the dancing makes her laugh and the drinks make her laugh harder.

So now she's here, sitting in one of those cushy circular booths that feels so nice against her butt and watching Gail, Sharon, Deb, and Carol do some ridiculous gyrations that are supposed to be sexy but are instead hilarious. 'Grinding,' she thinks they call it.

But Pam doesn't like dancing, not in the crushing heat of bodies, most of them twenty Earth-years their juniors, and the sweet thing is the other ladies don't make fun of her for it. They stop by between songs to make sure Pam is all right, and Pam is grateful for a little time apart. And now, tonight, June joins her because dancing like this is one Earth custom she prefers observing from a distance rather than partaking in.

Pam leans toward June. "What?"

"I said, 'Why didn't I like you ladies for a long time?'"

"Oh." Pam smiles, thinks, then says, "Probably internalized misogyny."

June doesn't know what the heck that means, but she's determined to go home and Giggle it.

She sips her neon-pink drink through an equally pink straw.

No. Wait. That's not right.

She sips again.

Google it.

"No, Deb," June says after swallowing a gulp of mimosa.

She's been coming to Sunday brunches with the gals for five weeks now, and she can-*not* get enough. Why do human beings limit themselves to brunch on only one day of the week? That's illogical. Earth women really do make delicious drinks, though. Who would've thought? And the drinks alone are worth coming back every week for.

"Listen, honey," June said, "he doesn't respect you. You can't keep taking him back because he gives you the eyes of a small dog."

Pam lays a hand on June's forearm. "Puppy, darling."

"Right, the eyes of a puppy. He's just going to whiz and crap on the carpet as soon as your back is turned."

"And by that, she means cheat on you again and break your heart," Sharon says.

"Thank you, Sharon." June snags the passing waitress. "May I have another of these delightful orange drinks that are actually yellow? Thank you so much. You have such lovely nostrils, by the way."

The woman laughs.

"He's been treating you like crap for years," Gail says. "Respect yourself because he's not going to do it for you."

"I think you should kick him to the curb," Pam says. "Make him come crawling back on his knees and then kick him to the curb again."

"Yeah, we'll have your back," Sharon says. "Anything you need."

Deb puts a hand over her heart. "You ladies . . . I just don't know how I can thank you for being so supportive. I think it's time."

"For?" Carol prompts, drawing out the word.

Deb breathes in deeply. She lets the breath out in a whoosh and says, "For a divorce." Then she covers her mouth, eyes wide as she giggles.

The table explodes in laughter. The waitress brings them a fifth round of mimosas. Mi-MO-sa. Such a lovely word. It rolls off the human tongue.

"What is that saying again?" June asks. She scrunches her nose up in thought. "The one I like so much but can never seem to remember?"

Gail leans forward and lowers her voice. "Eff the gosh-darn patriarchy."

"Oh, yes!" June says, not bothering to match her friend's pitch. "Fuck the goddamn patriarchy!" And she swallows her mimosa in a single gulp.

Moon Flowers

You enter the shop without meaning to. It calls, and you go, sending the bell above the door tinkling in the dead of the night. Out of the establishments open at this time—seedy bars, the odd twenty-four-hour grocery store or laundromat—it's certainly the most interesting. The mingled scents, dizzying and abundant, assault you as you walk in. Flowers fill your sight. Tables of them, coolers of them, vases bursting with them. Colors everywhere, brightening the darkness with a splash of the rainbow. Melancholy piano music plays through the speakers.

A woman—she's young, thoughtful-looking— appears from the back room to take up her place at the counter. "Welcome to Moon Flowers. Can I help you?"

Moon Flowers. How appropriate. How lovely. How magical.

Your mouth stutters open and closed and open again because you walked in for a reason and yet you cannot recall what it was. Perhaps it was simply to take pleasure in this oasis, this dreamland. "I came to browse," you finally say.

The woman nods as if this happens every night, a stranger walks into a flower shop at three AM just to look around at the blooms. "Of course. I'll be here if you decide you need help." She slides a paperback onto the counter and cracks it open.

You meander around, your steps slow and deliberate. Fairy lights hang around the perimeter of the ceiling. An orange tabby cat lies on a window ledge, lazily flicking its tail. An analog clock on the wall near the door ticks, its second hand stuttering, refusing to move forward.

Time stops.

You continue.

Tulips, chrysanthemums, marigolds, daffodils, roses, daisies inhabit vases all around you. More flowers you can't name surround you, like your own private garden. You sniff them all. If three AM isn't a time to stop and smell the roses, when is?

After inhaling the particularly fragrant aroma of honeysuckle, it occurs to you that you should purchase something. You've been in here for nearly twenty minutes, and no other customers have arrived. If you're going to take up this woman's time, the least you can do is make it worthwhile.

She's sitting contentedly on a stool, reading. Her glasses have slipped down her nose. A picture of quiet endearment.

Your heart palpitates erratically. You're afraid to break the silence, break the atmosphere. "Excuse me," you say.

She looks up.

"What's your favorite flower, by chance?"

She regards you for a moment before placing a bookmark in her novel and closing it. "Heather."

"Hmm." Your gaze darts around because the name sounds familiar but you can't place the actual flower.

Helpfully, she comes onto the main shop floor and points out sprigs of feathery purple flowers.

"Ah. What does it mean?" you ask.

"Floriography doesn't mean anything, actually," she says, her fingers brushing the petals. "The Victorians made it up."

"Isn't everything, to a certain extent, made up?"

"Three AM is no time for philosophy," she says.

"Says the woman who keeps her flower shop open from—" You squint at the sign on the wall behind the counter. "—dusk to dawn."

She lifts her eyebrows in a touché gesture. Instead of answering, she asks, "What's your favorite?"

"I don't have one. That's why I asked you. So I can buy something."

"You don't have to. Browsing is fine. After midnight, it's more common than buying."

"I'd like to."

She walks back around the counter. "What brings you here at this hour anyway?"

"Insomnia."

"What have you tried so far?"

"Everything. My current tactic is to take post-midnight walks through the city, which, you know, not the safest."

She purses her lips. "I have tea that might help. Do you want to try it?"

"Please."

"Give me a few minutes." Her eyes sparkle. "Perhaps in the meantime, you'll find a favorite."

You nod, watching her disappear into the back. You stuff your hands in the pockets of your hoodie. As ways to pass the time go, this isn't such an unpleasant one. Looks nicer than you, smells nicer than you. You could work here, escape the hell that is your current job. You could befriend this quiet girl, borrow her paperbacks and loan her some of your own.

You run a finger along a felty leaf. Better yet, you could build your own. You could buy a decent plot of land, build a greenhouse with a little annex for your living quarters. It seems to you that gardens, greenhouses, flower shops—wherever florae congregate—are havens of calm. You could live in that calm, nurture green to life and let it nurture you right back.

You inhale the heady aroma of the gardenias. You should've majored in botany. Maybe you still could. What's another fifty grand in student loans?

"So, have you chosen one?"

You jump at her voice. Instinctively, you point straight in front of you.

"Roses?" she asks, disappointment in her voice, as she sets a tea tray on the counter.

"Too predictable?"

She shrugs, noncommittal. "What color?"

"Mm . . ." You point to a cluster of lavender petals.

"Now, that's more interesting."

You saunter forward, lean on the counter. "How so?"

"Lavender means enchantment," she says, pouring two cups of steaming tea. "I suppose the question now is what—or whom—will be the source of such enchantment?"

"Oh, nothing, I imagine," you say because despite the unreality of this late hour, it's true. You run through a list of your life's big bullet points—an unfulfilling job, no close friends unless you count the guy at the pizza shop down the road, a crappy apartment that won't allow pets, unbeatable insomnia. Yeah, no enchantment on the radar.

"Well," she says before taking a sip of tea. "Perhaps that's what you've been called here to find out."

You glance up at the sign again to make sure this is just a flower shop, not some kind of woo-

woo New Agey place that plies you with a free palm reading to rope you into a monthly healing crystal subscription that costs more than your rent. Not that there's anything wrong with that. Except the part where you can barely pay rent to begin with. But maybe that's the point of the crystals . . .

She gestures to the untouched mug then slides around the counter. You drink. The first sip dances on your tongue. Warmth spreads from your chest to your stomach to your legs.

Oh, daaaamn.

You could fall asleep right now on this pillow of coziness and soft light.

Closing your eyes, you inhale cinnamon and cloves in the steam and sip again. Your head fogs pleasantly, and the world slows as the shop owner gathers a bundle of the roses. She ties them up with a pale pink ribbon.

"How much do I owe you?" you ask, reaching sluggishly for your wallet.

She thumbs at the corner of her paperback. "What are you willing to give? Your insomnia, maybe?"

Your mind's a little slow at the moment, but you think—you're pretty certain—that's a strange answer. It's uncool to combat questions with questions. Terribly uncool.

Before your tongue can wrap around those words though, much less those words in politer form, she smiles. "Just a little late-night humor. Sorry. That'll be twenty-one nineteen."

You hand over a twenty and a five and stuff the change into a tip jar wrapped in burlap with an evergreen sprig sticking out of it. An extra push gets the words, "Thanks for the tea," out of your mouth.

She nods solemnly, her smile small again. Still there, though. "You're welcome."

"So, goodnight."

"Goodnight."

And just like that, your feet are carrying you out of this weird, amazing little place. You twiddle your fingers at the tabby in the window, and they're curled around the brass doorknob when the shopkeeper's soft voice rings out.

"Solitude."

You turn. "What's that?"

"Heather. It represents solitude."

You feel like you should note this information somehow, tuck it into a dark pocket of your brain, stuck safely between your childhood best friend's birthday and your grandma's apple pie recipe, and maybe it gets in there or maybe it dissipates into the fog. Either way, you don't remember the walk home at all. All you remember is the bouquet clutched in your fist, the streetlights blotting out the stars, the floating feeling in your legs, and the gentle impact of your head against the pillow.

The roses live in a plastic souvenir cup from a baseball game, filled halfway with water, in the corner of the kitchen counter, where they become a little bright spot in your dull world. The sight of them evokes a smile in the morning when you get up and in the evening when you come home from work. Otherwise, you don't pay them much attention.

Until one evening you're in your dinosaur pajamas eating Cocoa Krispies for dinner and staring at the bouquet. You pause, spoon halfway to your mouth and dripping milk, because you haven't watered those suckers.

Like, at all.

Time means little when you don't sleep much.

Except . . . Except you *have* slept. You've slept very well. For three weeks or so, actually.

It's been three weeks, and those lavender roses you haven't watered since the night a mysterious shop owner gave them to you are still kicking.

So, that's not weird at all.

You put it out of your mind until you can't, so . . . twenty minutes. Your willpower's never been very strong. You throw on sneakers and your college sweatshirt and are out the door the moment the sun goes down.

The whole walk to Moon Flowers, you clutch your phone and contemplate calling your mom. She likes to garden, always remembers the names of flowers and whether they're annuals or perennials. Meanwhile, you still can't remember the difference between the two. Annuals sound like they should come up every year, don't they?

You should call your mom because she'll know whether roses are supposed to last three weeks and could stop you from looking like a complete fool.

As if your pajama pants don't do that already.

Oh, this is ridiculous. You are being ridiculous. But a girl gave you magic flowers and magic tea and cured your insomnia and you'd rather be ridiculous than ignorant. You'd rather look foolish trying to thank her for something she's not responsible for than be an ass by *not* thanking her for something she *is* responsible for.

Right?

You're in dinosaurs pajamas on your way to a magic flower shop.

You don't even know anymore.

Maybe you never did.

What you do know is this:

Standing in the middle of the sidewalk, you stare at a whitewashed door nestled between a bar and a laundromat, a door you swear had a bundle of alyssum hanging from it only weeks prior. No fairy lights shining through the window. No creepy piano music muffled by the old wood. No enigmatic, nocturnal shop owner offering strange tea brews.

After pounding—gently, it is late, after all—on the door for a few minutes, you ask your phone for the address of Moon Flowers on Whistler Street, and the cool female reply confirms that no, you don't even know:

The establishment you have requested does not exist.

Seven months later, you move out of your crappy apartment and into a nicer one closer to your new job, your better job, your job that means vacations and little splurges and no more headaches about school loan payments.

Your belongings don't fill many boxes. One for the kitchen. One for your clothes. Two for your books. Even so, you pack the roses last. As you settle them into a tall box that will nestle between the seats of your car, you wonder where they came from.

The Planet of Purple Forests

The cell is dark. No windows. But Jae can generally keep track of the time by the relative strength of her hunger. That—and the fact that all nine of her cellmates are asleep in their bunks— means it's night. The middle of.

She doesn't sleep much anymore, though. She lies on her back, one arm stretched behind her head and the other tossing a small rubber ball toward the ceiling. Even in the darkness, her aim is good. One night, though, she'll drop it straight on her face. Not tonight, the seventeenth night of her imprisonment behind enemy lines.

Whatever that means. She's not even sure who the enemy is anymore.

The lock clicks.

She sits up and shields her eyes from the light that streams in from the hallway. Then the overhead light buzzes to life, and her cellmates—her soldiers—are stirring into consciousness.

"Everyone, up!" the jailer bellows.

The translator implanted in Jae's left ear means she hears it in her own language. Before her imprisonment, the Karv language had been a nuisance, something she couldn't get the hang of. Now, she sort of misses the musicality of it. Odd how easy it is to take a thing for granted. She stows the rubber ball away in one of her boots, lying just beneath the cot, awaiting morning, and she's the first on her feet, the first to stand at the foot of her bed—bare soles against the cold metal floor, chin high, arms clasped behind her back. Across the aisle, Zeke struggles not to sway as he wipes the sleep from his eyes. A curse forms on his lips, and Jae smirks. He was always the last of their squad up every morning.

Then the expression falls. Because it's her fault they're prisoners of war. No matter at whose door the blame for this bloodshed rests, that one's on her. Leading her soldiers into ambush for the sake of her conscience.

When all ten are lined up, sloppily so, along their bunks, the jailer waves to someone waiting in the corridor.

Someones, actually. Three people stride in. The first two are dressed in drab gray uniforms with the crest of their planet on their breasts. Foot soldiers and guards. How many uniforms like that has she bloodied? Too many to keep track of.

Jae's breath catches in her throat because the last person isn't wearing the gray of a common recruit. There's a gun at her hip, and she wears black trousers, shiny black boots, and a crimson vest over a crisp black shirt. The vest is unadorned, but this person is important. The only questions are why she's visiting them and why in the middle of the night. Whatever the answers, they can't be good. So Jae keeps her head up and her gaze straight ahead as the woman moves down the line, inspecting them.

Of all the places Jae imagined ending up, a prisoner-of-war camp on an alien planet wasn't one of them. But after college, money was scarce. Not in the military, though. So she donned a uniform and has been eating three square meals a day since. Even in this place, which, for a prison, isn't horrible. Still, she'll probably get killed here, and all because the military promised a future without loans hanging over her head like the sword of Damocles.

When the woman reaches her, Jae calms herself by thinking about how much this doesn't matter, not really. They're at war, and war isn't fair or good or honorable. This inspection is probably pinpointing the weakest link, the one who will break first, the one who will divulge Earth secrets at the merest threat of torture.

It'll be Pasternack. Of course it will be. And a quick flick of her gaze over to the young, pimple-faced soldier is enough to know that he realizes it, too. And when that moment comes, Jae will volunteer to take his place. After all, they wouldn't be here if not for her.

What Jae doesn't expect, though, is the way this woman smells—woodsy, like pine and sap and fresh air. Human, almost. It shouldn't surprise her because the Karvs look human enough. The prevailing theory is that Karvs and Earth humans share a common ancestor, but it's not her job to science. It's her job to shoot.

So, no, the smell shouldn't surprise her, but it does and she jerks and her gaze abruptly meets this woman's. Her eyes are a vibrant purple, darker than the eyes of the other Karv that Jae's met. Jae lets her gaze follow the woman around the room until she's gotten a good look at all ten of them and stands once more by the jailer and her guards at the entranceway.

Jae holds her breath as the woman tips her head in Jae's direction and, voice low and scratchy, says, "That one."

Jae lets out her breath. At least it wasn't Pasternack. Before she can react, the guards are grabbing her by the elbows and frog-marching her out. Zeke's eyes widen with terror.

"Wait," Jae says, stupidly. "My boots." Also her clothes. She's in cotton shorts and her camo-green t-shirt.

"You won't need them," says the woman.

Jae gulps, not caring to know what that means. They form a strange little procession—the mysterious woman in the front and Jae between the guards in the back. She walks along with them instead of resisting. That can be her first move of protest, should she need it, and besides, she'd rather not stub her toes. She's going to need them for running.

"Where are you taking me?" she asks.

No response. Not that she'd expected one, but she likes to know up front if she's definitely going to be tortured. She likes to be mentally prepared.

"You don't have to torture me, you know," she says. She could take it; she just isn't in the mood right now. "We can negotiate."

The woman stops walking and turns, making the guards drag Jae to a halt, too.

"What makes you think we're going to torture you?" the woman asks. She looks almost offended.

Maybe Jae's been wrong. Maybe there is some honor in war, at least on the part of the Karv. After all, she's been treated decently so far. Why should things change now?

Jae swallows, and her voice is cowed when she says, "You pulled me out of my bunk in the middle of the night, and now you're dragging me down the halls. I was just working out the logical conclusion."

The woman's brow furrows. "It's late because I was busy." Then her brow clears and sarcasm creeps into her voice. "Apologies for not running on your typical schedule, Sergeant."

It's only another minute before they lead her into an intrabuilding transport box. It's similar to an elevator back on Earth, but it runs along multiple axes. When the transport stops, they emerge into a hallway that looks the same as all the others—metal and octagonal with strips of lights down each panel.

Fifty or so meters down the hall, they stop in front of a door. The guards' grips loosen.

The woman presses buttons on the access panel until the door opens and then gestures inside. "Your room," she says. "Wash up, and get a good night's sleep. I'll be back for you in the morning."

The guards take their hands away completely, leaving Jae alone, like they have no care whether she makes a break for it instead of ducking into the room. Not that she'd make it out of this compound. It's a maze, and not one she has knowledge of.

"Wait," she calls.

The woman turns back.

"Why?"

"Excuse me?"

"Why are you doing all this?" Jae gestures to herself. "And why just me? Why not the rest of my squad?"

"The queen wishes to speak to someone from Earth, to learn of your ways and what it will take to negotiate for peace," the woman says. "You're the highest ranking officer we have access to."

Jae stifles a snort. If she's the highest they've got, they must not have many at all. She'd assumed they were one of numerous cells, but maybe not.

"Besides," the woman says, her gaze on the floor panels as a soft smile tugs at her lips. "You have an honest face."

All three Karv turn and stride down the corridor. When they've turned a corner, Jae ducks through the narrow door into an octagonal room. Behind her, the door closes with a pneumatic *hiss*. A giant circular bed sits in the center of the room. A thick red duvet and soft red sheets are draped over it, and the middle features a pile of white pillows. No windows, but the walls are lined with screens that, upon further inspection, will show her anything she desires. For now, she leaves them black.

There's a desk to her left and a bookshelf to her right. Each shelf is packed with books, most in the Karv language, but there are others in languages unrecognizable to Jae.

In the back of the room, directly across from the door to the hallway, lies another door, this one to the washroom. Jae lets out a surprised laugh at the sight. In addition to an honest-to-Earth toilet, there's a round tub big enough for eight people and a giant square shower with multiple jet streams and faucets protruding from the walls and ceiling. It's more luxury than she's seen in years, and she's not one to look a gift horse in the mouth, even if it comes from her enemy.

She strips out of her sleepwear and tosses them on the tile floor. She fiddles with the shower controls until she achieves an almost scalding temperature. Once she steps in and closes the door, she turns on the wall jets. She groans. The hot, pressurized water reminds her it's been much too long since she's been totally at ease. Comfort is for the privileged—which she isn't; she's merely a pawn in a game where she can't see the whole board—but she can pretend for just a night.

The water never goes cold. She stays under the spray for at least thirty minutes, letting it knead out the knots in her overworked muscles. She'd stay here forever if she could, but she's starting to get wrinkly, so, reluctantly, she turns off the water and steps out. As she drips, the tile flooring absorbs the water. A panel in the wall opens, and a bar emerges, a fluffy blue towel hanging from its end. She rubs herself down, and when she's dry, a panel just below the first one slides open to offer a long-sleeved shirt and pants of indeterminate material that are, nevertheless, astonishingly soft. She may be a hardened soldier, but she could get used to this.

Back in the main room, she moves a few pillows from the center of the bed to the end then folds down the duvet and crawls beneath the sheets. Her body sinks into the bed in a way that makes her feel cradled, cocooned. As she closes her eyes, the lights lining the perimeter of the ceiling fade and then go out altogether. And despite her recent bout of insomnia, she's asleep in minutes.

The morning comes with a gentle flickering of the perimeter lights until, when Jae opens her eyes, they stay on steadily. It's like the room knows exactly what's happening inside her body. Maybe the implant in her ear isn't simply a translator. In her refreshed state, she can't really bring herself to care. She's been better taken care of here than she was among her own army, so if they're keeping track of her vitals, then they're doing a damn good job of it.

The screens greet her with a peaceful scene of the tide lapping against the shore. It looks familiar enough that it could be Earth, almost like it wants to remind her of home, set her at ease even more than she already has been. Groaning, she sinks back into the mattress, thinks about home. It's been so long since she left it behind, since she saw it last that she's not even sure if she can call it home anymore.

You can't go home again. Isn't that the phrase? If she got shipped back today, would there be anything left for her? Her squad is her family. She's got none left on Earth. Anything else she'd go back for—a little home to herself in a solitary corner of the world, nice views, peace and quiet—she can find here. A little different, of course. Blue beaches instead of white ones. Purple forests instead of green. The stars are as incredible as always, though.

After a minute, the lights start to blink. She drags herself out of the luxurious bed and into the bathroom. It's summer, or what passes for it on this planet, and the compound is kept at a relatively warm temperature, but the floor tiles are heated, and blessedly so. Just the thing her chilly morning feet need.

She goes through her routine, brushing her teeth and washing her face and all the rest, and then the wall wardrobe opens to offer clothing for the day. Black pants, soft and flowy. Cotton socks and supple boots. A fresh-smelling white shirt with a toothless zipper from the collar down to the middle. And a lightweight, embroidered black coat.

Once she's dressed and her boots laced up, a chime sounds.

"Uh . . . Yes?"

The door to her room opens, allowing the woman from last night to step in. "The queen is ready for you. This way."

Good morning to you, too, Jae thinks as she adjusts the sleeves of her coat. Nevertheless, she follows the woman into the hallway. Once they've turned a few corners and it's clear the other woman isn't going to open the conversation, Jae asks, "How did you sleep?"

"Is that necessary information for you?" the woman asks.

Not necessary at all. No small talk ever is. "On my planet, it's a polite thing to ask in the morning."

"Oh," the woman says, still looking ahead. "I slept well."

When no responding question comes, Jae snorts quietly.

"What? Did I answer incorrectly?" the woman asks.

"No. It was fine," Jae says. "But we didn't exactly hit it off last night." She sticks her hand out and introduces herself.

"I know who you are, Sergeant."

Jae plants herself. "And yet I don't know who you are, and I don't take kindly to being at a disadvantage."

As the woman sighs, Jae gets the distinct impression she's refraining from rolling her eyes. But even though she refuses the handshake, she says, "My name is Persey."

"It's nice to meet you, Persey." And it is. She's not just being cheeky. It's nice because prisoners are non-entities and this is the first real, human-ish contact she's had in weeks. She's been too guilt-ridden over their capture that she hasn't let her squad in, not really.

Persey holds Jae's gaze for a few breaths longer than necessary. "Are you ready now, Sergeant?"

"Lead the way."

Soon, the metal passageways of the compound morph into stone. It's like they're walking through layers of the world itself. Then the stone turns to wood, beautiful purple wood harvested from the planet itself. It's unlike anything Jae's seen, unlike anything she's imagined. The different grains of wood present in varying shades until the whole walls are awash with color. All point to a high, transparent ceiling—glass, perhaps, but it almost seems as if nothing's there at all—that allows a stunning view of the sky. How wondrous this room must be at night. Now, orange sunlight streams in, warming Jae's face. She gasps at the beauty of the scene.

"Do you like it?" Persey asks quietly, a smirk at the corner of her mouth.

Jae can only nod. Bloodshed and pain, the coldness of metal, the terror of war—those are what she's seen of this world. This, though, is inner Karv. This is the truth of their people. Jae is blessed to simply lay her eyes upon it.

"What is it?" she asks in a whisper.

"This room? It's the queen's hall," Persey says.

"No, the wood. The trees it's harvested from."

"They are the yaganod. It's a family of trees, each species boasts a slightly different hue."

"It's incredible," Jae breathes.

"Does it not seem wrong to you?"

"What? Why would it seem wrong?" How could something this beautiful be wrong?

"I've seen holograms of your Earth. The forests there are green and brown."

"No," Jae says, shaking her head, "your world is different. That's all. Not wrong. Nor is mine right."

Persey's step falters—so slightly Jae thinks her eyes might have tricked her.

At the end of the vast hall, past a circular wooden table, is a throne carved out of the same lumber, but the purple tinges into black at the ends of the fingers that protrude from the back of the chair. A woman sits, assured and regal. Deep furrows line a face that's seen too much.

Overcome—with fear, with awe, with something—Jae drops to one knee and bends her head. Whatever will follow this moment will change her life forever. All she can do as she waits for the queen to speak is hope the coming change is to her benefit.

The quiet room fills with the sound of the queen's hearty chuckle, and when Jae chances a glance up, both the queen and Persey are smiling.

"Rise, Sergeant," says the queen. "That is not necessary."

Jae stands. Hands folded behind her back, she waits.

The queen stands, too, and, leaning on a wooden cane, steps down from the dais. The queen's eyes are the same deep purple as Persey's, lovely in a way that makes Jae want to know more—about the person, about the people, about the planet. There's an entire new world here—not new to the Karv, but new to her—and instead of exploring, of forging new alliances, her people have started a war over a land they know nothing of.

The queen makes a slow, deliberate circle around her, and Jae's chest heaves as she endeavors to control her breathing. Once again, she is under scrutiny. Only this time, she's had a full night's sleep in a comfortable bed to help her stand up under it.

The queen completes her circuit and comes to a stop in front of Jae. She's a head shorter, so Jae has to tilt her chin down to meet her eyes.

"You were right. Her face is honest," the queen says to Persey. Turning back to Jae, she asks, "Are you hungry?"

Very much so, and Jae has seen nothing in the behavior of either of these women to suggest they'd withhold a meal from her simply because she's hungry, so she tells the truth. "Yes, ma'am."

The queen's smile wrinkles her face even further. "Good. Food warms the belly and opens pathways to the mind. Come, then."

She leads them into an antechamber, a much smaller room with screens instead of windows, the same screens that featured in Jae's borrowed room. Here, they portray views of the sky at night, stars dotting the darkness, galactic swirls of reds and purples. If she doesn't pay attention to the fact that none of the constellations are recognizable, it almost looks like the night sky on Earth.

The queen sits at the head of a small rectangular table, where place settings and food are already laid out. Some of it's familiar to Jae—staples like squishy orange bread and brown protein cubes—but the rest looks fancier than anything she was given as a prisoner. Persey pulls out a chair for Jae to the queen's left before sitting at the queen's other hand.

"Forgive me . . . Your Majesty," Jae says, uncertain of how she should address the monarch, if at all. When Persey gives her a small nod, she continues, "What is it you want from me, exactly?"

The queen takes a bite of a cake-looking item, chews thoughtfully, and finally swallows before saying, "What is it like on your planet? Do Terrans train from birth? Are you born into a class of soldiers?"

"Terrans, ma'am?"

"It's what we call your people," Persey says.

"Oh, um, no, ma'am," Jae says. The mug at her right hand is filled with a green liquid that's surprisingly sweet. "We can choose what we do to earn a living. Before I was a soldier, I was a student." At blank looks from the other two, she adds, "A scholar."

"Oh. Someone who fights with their mind as well as their body," the queen says, sitting back in her chair and interlocking her fingers. "You're a very good choice, indeed."

Jae toys with a fork-like utensil. Praise is nice, and different, but a good choice for what?

"Why did you give it up?" Persey asks softly. "Scholarship."

"Oh, um, I couldn't afford it."

"Affor—?" Persey's eyebrows rise. "They make you pay for education?" she asks, upper lip slightly curled as if the thought disgusts her. "What good does that do? Isn't it available to everyone?"

"Not really, no," Jae says. "Or they tell us it is, but then we spend most of our lives paying them back."

The Karv are quiet, Persey stewing in anger while the queen looks contemplative.

"What would you do?" the queen asks. "If you didn't have to repay the money for your education and you could be something other than a soldier?"

Jae spreads a bright blue substance on her bread while she thinks. "All I want, really, is a quiet life. I might be a farmer. Maybe have some goats." The thought makes her smile, but the smile turns to a grimace. "But I am in debt, and there is a war on. I can't let myself think about a possibility that might never happen."

The queen smiles. "Then be my ambassador."

"What?" An ambassador? An ambassador has to be clever and cunning and everything she isn't. "No. No, I couldn't."

"Why not?"

"I'm a soldier, not a diplomat."

"Of course you're a diplomat," the queen says. "We all are. The only difference is the scale of the problems we each face. You're accustomed to dealing with disputes among the soldiers you're in charge of, are you not?"

Jae nods.

"Then I'm asking you to use those same skills, only on a much larger scale."

Jae gulps the sweet green drink to force down the lump in her throat. She can lead a few soldiers, sure, but she's no commander of nations. How will she get anyone to even listen to her?

When she looks up, Persey is regarding her with curiosity.

"Why?" Jae asks. "Why do you need an ambassador?"

The queen's gaze is steady yet soft. "How else are we to achieve peace?"

Jae straightens her shoulders. Peace. Peace would mean her people could return to their families. Peace would mean she could carve out a place for herself here, on this world. Peace would mean no more blood on her hands.

Even if war is without honor, it seems this queen might have enough to save them all.

"If you do this for me," the queen says, "I will take your debt on."

"What?"

"When you help me negotiate a peace with your people, you will have no debt and, therefore, no reason to stay a soldier. You may do whatever you like."

Jae, suddenly, is lightheaded. That would be complete freedom. A laugh bubbles up in her throat because she wouldn't even know what to do with such freedom.

"Is that a yes?" asks the queen.

The Karv can't do this on their own, nor can the people of Earth. They have to do this together, and if Jae can help facilitate that, then doesn't she at least have to try? "Yes," she says. "I'll be your ambassador."

"Good. We haven't much time. You leave for your people's military base in two days."

Two days? How much could she possibly learn about Karv in two days?

The queen stands. "If you'll excuse me, I have a council to attend. I will meet you in the library after supper tonight for a lesson on Earth. I want to know everything and anything that could help me craft an offer they'll listen to. Until then, Persey will answer any questions you have about our people and our home."

Before Jae can nod, the queen retreats into the hall, and through the open door, Jae catches a glimpse of the table, its seats now filled with bodies.

"Is that the queen's council?" she asks.

"Yes," says Persey.

"There is only one man on it."

That draws a smirk from Persey. "The queen is of the opinion that men have neither the temperament nor the discipline for politics and negotiation."

Jae laughs lightly through her nose. That's true from her own experience, too. Even if the women on her planet recognize that, which they do, the men in charge won't give up their power that easily, not when they're still arguing about women being "too emotional" for leadership. "And what about you? Do you agree with her?" she asks Persey.

"I've found that, more often than not, she's correct."

Jae lets the silence wash over them, listens to the muffled murmurings from the council hall. An ambassador. That assumes her superiors will even listen to her.

"You're going to be remarkable, Sergeant," Persey says. "How did you eat?"

Jae's chuckle is wet, through held-back tears. "Very well, thank you."

Jae's hands shake as Persey escorts her to the land transport, the slender, armored vehicle that will take Jae across the disputed zones and into the territory humans have claimed for themselves. This is so much responsibility, too much responsibility. She can't do this. She can't carry the weight of a civilization—of two civilizations—on her shoulders. She's stooping and bending already, and by the time she reaches her own people, she'll break.

"You can do this," Persey says, voice gentle.

Jae turns to face her. "And if I can't?"

"Then we learn from our mistakes and we try again." Persey smiles. "All right?"

"All right," Jae says. She doesn't quite believe it, but if she repeats it to herself on the trip, maybe she will. She hefts the bag on her shoulder.

"Before you go," Persey says, reaching into the pocket of her jacket and retrieving a figure carved from the purple wood native to this planet. She holds it in her open palm. It's got four legs, floppy ears, and a shaggy coat. "I researched what a goat is. I'm not sure I got it quite right," she says, looking down and twisting her fingers in the hem of her shirt.

Jae chuckles as she accepts the gift. "It's incredible. Thank you."

Persey takes a step backward. "I believe it's the custom of Earth to wish you well, and so I wish you well."

"Same to you," Jae says as she climbs into the transport.

"Goodbye, Sergeant Cabrera."

"Goodbye . . ." Jae stops because she doesn't know Persey's surname. She doesn't even know if the Karv have surnames. That's something she wants to live long enough to return and find out. "Goodbye, Persey."

Then the door closes, and the transport engulfs her.

When Jae arrives at her own military camp and steps out of the transport, the faces of her fellow soldiers are slack with surprise. A group comes running toward her, surrounding her with shouts and questions.

"But you're MIA!"

"Where are the rest of your men?"

"And where'd you get one of these vehicles?"

"What's that in your ear?"

"We assumed . . ."

Yeah, they assumed she was dead. She doesn't blame them. If their roles were reversed, she would've thought the same thing. Still, the questioning is more suspicious than curious.

"Can we go inside?" she asks. "I'll explain everything in there. To the general. I need to speak with him."

Their base is less permanent, more haphazard than the Karvs'. It's made of melded-together spare parts and anything they could scavenge from the surrounding planetside. But not in the way the Karv harvest it. Not in a way that leaves the land anything but decimated. The sight pinches Jae's heart, but then she's being led inside and there's no more time to think about it because all she can think about is getting the queen's message of peace to the general.

They march her into a bay where a man in a white jumpsuit tells her to take off her jacket and roll up her sleeve.

"Why?" she asks.

"Just a blood sample. It's standard," a guard says.

"Standard for what, exactly?" Jae asks as she pulls her arm away from the medic, who huffs and looks at the guard for help.

"Whenever someone's had contact with them," the guard says. "Have to test for diseases."

"Karv."

"What?"

"That's what they're called. Not 'them.'"

The guard *pfts*. "Fine. Karv. You could've brought back diseases, and we're not endangering this whole base." He grips her wrist, hard, and holds her arm out straight. "Now let the good doctor take a blood sample."

Jae complies. Reluctantly. But the sooner she gets an audience with the general, the sooner she can return home.

The medic jabs the needle in, but the shock of that thought eclipses the pain. Home. She's found a home, of sorts, with the Karv. What does that mean? What does that make her?

When the sample's taken and the medic's taped a ball of gauze to her elbow, she shrugs on her jacket and says, "I need a line to the general."

The guard laughs. Then he sobers. "You're serious?"

"Yeah. And I need that line now."

Eleven separate men explain why, exactly, it is that she can't get a line to the general. All eleven excuses are different, but all eleven are bullshit. The more time they waste, though, the more people will die in this bloody war—Terrans and Karv. And so, right in the middle of the eleventh excuse, she gets up, marches out of the room, and storms through the compound. She's vaguely aware of men flapping and fluttering behind her, but peace is a mantra in her heart, driving her.

Finally, she lands right in a situation room. Over twenty men—all of ranks higher than hers, much higher—sit around a large metal table. Their heads turn toward her in unison when she bangs the doors open. On the opposite wall is a giant screen, which they're using to conference with the—

"General!" she shouts.

The general on the screen blinks and looks toward the men around the table. "Who is this? How did she get in here?"

"Sir, my name's Sergeant Jae Cabrera. I was captured by the Karv weeks ago, but their queen sent for me to tell her about our people, our ways. And she told me about hers." The guards are on her now, dragging her out by her elbows. "She wants peace, sir. She wants peace!"

The dragging stops, though the guards don't release their vise-grips on her arms. The arguing and indistinct voices she hasn't been paying attention to all cease at the same moment. There's a long pause, during which Jae swears her heart is going to burst from nerves, and then the general is asking for privacy and everyone else in the room is filing out until she's alone.

She's alone with the highest-ranking general in the Terran army, and she's responsible for convincing him to work toward peace.

Breathe, Cabrera. Just breathe.

His face softens. "Sit, please, and tell me your story."

She does, and each word builds her hope that she can do this, that they can achieve amity. When she's done, when she takes a deep breath and looks up at the screen, the general doesn't look pleased.

"Sergeant," he says, his voice raw from years of smoking, "it's easy to see what's happened here."

It is? She swallows, finding her throat suddenly dry. She grabs at a glass of water left behind by one of the men and downs half of it before the general continues.

"I know the Karv," he says. "I know how they work, how they manipulate us. They kept you in that cell for weeks because they had to make you pliable. Likely, they did this through the food and drink they gave you. Not only did you think that you were being well taken care of, but they put a substance in it that made you . . . more amenable to their presence, shall we say?"

He's smirking. He's smirking, and she doesn't know why. Because none of this makes sense. She never hated the Karv, never felt repulsed in their presence, never wanted to kill them. She's just a soldier, and killing is what soldiers do.

"They earned your trust, artificially, of course," he says. "Then they made you believe in peace, made you believe it was achievable. And they sent you here not to convince me but to learn our secrets and take them back."

All her protests die on her tongue. She told the queen she wasn't cut out for this. She's not someone people listen to, not unless they have to, like the soldiers under her command. They tolerate her, barely respect her. Oh, hell, she's going to puke.

"They don't want peace, Sergeant. They want victory."

She finishes the rest of the water. She can't bring herself to look him in the eye. This is so far from the response she expected that she has no game plan now. She is numb.

"Now," he says calmly, "let me call for someone. They'll find you a room for the night, and you can recuperate."

What happens next passes in a blur. It's only when she's being shuffled out of the room that she realizes something.

The general has a dishonest face.

Jae can't sleep. She's a soldier; she should be able to sleep anywhere. Now, her insomnia comes from more than simple dissatisfaction with her life. It comes from longing for a bed as soft as the stars. It's more than the bed, though. She feels comfortable in that room. She feels comfortable in the presence of the Karv queen, the Karv people.

That scares her, in the way comfort can scare a person who has given up any prospect of home, but while it simply scares her, it angers the general.

She can't leave, not without anyone noticing, but she can go for a walk. She makes sure the carved goat Persey gave her is secure in her pocket and heads out the door, where she runs straight into a guard. Why are they keeping a guard on her door?

"Can I help you with something?" the guard asks.

Jae takes a steadying breath. "I wanted to take a walk."

The guard shakes his head.

"Fine, but I can't sleep. I just need to move, get out of that room."

He purses his lips together, weighing the options.

"Come on," she says. "You know what it's like. The nightmares. The claustrophobia. Twenty minutes is all I need."

"All right," he says through a heavy sigh. He waves his gun. "Now get going. I'm timing you, and you've already lost five seconds."

She's halfway down the darkened hall when he calls out, "You need the backpack with you?"

She flips him off and wanders the base, practicing deep breaths. What can she do now? Stay here, but that would be counterproductive for everyone involved. Go back to the queen and work on a new proposition to take to the general, but the general's not the type of person to rethink something. His answer is final, even though his answer is wrong.

She stops at the sound of voices. It's another few seconds before the voices resolve themselves into proper words.

"How long is the incubation period?" asks a man with a deep, gruff voice.

"Twelve hours," another, squeakier voice replies.

"Impressive."

There's shuffling—footsteps—and Jae turns around quickly

"Sergeant?" the first man asks. "What are you doing out of bed?"

She plasters a pleasant smile on her face before turning. "Couldn't sleep. Just need to get a little air."

He looks her up and down then nods. "Well, you get back to your bunk now. You've got a big day tomorrow."

"I do?"

"We're sending you back to the Karv."

"You took a blood sample the other day," Jae protests. "Surely nothing's changed in my biology in a few days that it warrants another test."

The medic doesn't look at her as he preps the needle. "I'm not taking your blood. I'm giving you a vaccine."

Jae jerks her arm away. "For what?"

"It's standard."

"That's not what I asked."

The exasperated medic looks to the guard, and Jae holds out her arm before the guard can manhandle her. She just wants to get out of here. She just wants to go home. If she has to do what they want so they send her back, then so be it.

This time, she feels the pinch of the needle as it goes under her skin.

"Welcome back," Persey says as soon as Jae steps from the transport.

Welcome home is what Jae hears.

The day after she returns to the palace of the Karv, Jae wakes with determination. She hadn't had a chance to tell the queen about the general's refusal, not when Persey had noticed the bags under her eyes, shuffled her off to her room, and sent for a hot meal, after which Jae had promptly fallen asleep, even without changing into her heavenly Karv pajamas. She wakes with every intention of informing the queen, and this is what occupies her mind as she strides out of her room and into an empty corridor.

Strange.

"Hello?" she calls. "Where is everyone?"

Normally, the place is bustling with people, even if the only ones she ever paid attention to were Persey and the queen. Fear winds its way through her gut, sharp and repugnant.

"Persey?"

She walks slowly through the metal section of the base, through the stone section, and finally into the wood section. All are eerily quiet. This isn't normal. This isn't right.

She moves through the throne room, through the antechamber where she'd eaten with the queen barely a week prior, and up a spiral staircase. She pauses at the top of it. This level, too, is silent.

She chances opening a door. Inside, half a dozen Karv lie on the ground or sit slumped in chairs, eyes wide open and unblinking.

She slams the door shut. They're sleeping. They're just sleeping.

Then a door at the end of the sunlit hallway creaks open.

Persey, carrying a basin of water, emerges. She stops short when she sees Jae.

"What's going on?" Jae asks, afraid of the answer. "What's happening? Where is everyone?"

Persey licks her lips. She looks down at the floor before meeting Jae's gaze again. "You better come on, then," she says and leads her into the room she'd just come from.

It's a bedroom, the queen's bedroom. The woman in question lies in bed, a trickle of dark purple blood at the corner of her mouth. As Persey sets the basin on a nearby table, the stained purple water sloshes.

Everything comes crashing down in an instant, and Jae falls to her knees. They let her go. She should've seen this coming. She should've seen it.

"What's happened to her?" she asks, arm extended toward the near-motionless woman in the bed. She draws back at the last moment.

Persey sits on the mattress. "The queen is sick, Sergeant."

Back to Sergeant, then.

"But it's not just the queen," Persey says.

Jae looks up. "What do you mean?"

"We're all sick."

Jae can see it now, see the sallow color of Persey's skin, the sweat on her brow, the sag of her shoulders.

"We're all . . ."

Dying, Jae finishes to herself, like the Karv in that room she'd looked into. Because this scenario isn't new. Because they knew her allegiance was slipping. Because she delivered a weapon into their hands and they took every advantage. Peace is a lie, and she believed it.

"What can I do?" she asks.

"What can be done? Nothing at all," Persey says. Her voice hardens as she adds, "Now you wait. You wait for us to die out. Then you dispose of our bodies like we're refuse, and you take everything we built. You take our cities, our homes, our crops. You take our planet like the monsters you are."

"I didn't—" She didn't have anything to do with this, is what Jae wants to say. But it's not the truth. She *did* have something to do with it, even if she didn't mean to, even if she didn't know. "I never meant for this to happen. I swear it."

Persey's eyes, once alive and vibrant, are cold.

"Persey," the queen says, reaching out. Her voice is weak.

Persey clasps the queen's hand. "I'm here. I'm here, My Queen. What do you need?"

"Take my implant out, Persey."

"What?"

The queen looks directly at Jae. "I want to hear the traitor, truly hear her voice as she tells me our fate."

Tears fill Jae's eyes. The queen wants to hear the true language of the people who have killed her, destroyed her culture, eliminated her people's futures. "I'm sorry," she tries again. "I didn't know this was going to happen. I . . ."

But Persey is right. There's nothing she can say to fix this, so she says nothing as she sits with them for hours.

The queen goes first and with her, Jae's new world. As it crumbles around her, each cascade shakes her body. Before she knows it, Persey has lain down beside the fallen queen. Jae kneels at her side.

"Tell me a lie," Persey says, her voice cracking. "A good one. One I can hold onto."

Jae brushes her hair back from her forehead. Leaning forward, she whispers, "Everything will be all right."

Soon, all too soon, Jae's quiet sobs are the only sound in the room. She stops holding back her tears, and they splash onto the bedsheets. The only thing she wants at this moment is to go back in time, reverse all the decisions she made that led here. But she had wanted peace, too, and look where that landed her.

When her tears are spent, she takes Persey's gun from her holster and hefts it in her palm. Persey would forgive her, she thinks. She hopes. She's one person, one Karv, and she won't be able to stop them, but when the Terrans come, she'll be ready.

A Whisper from the Waves

In a small town on the coast of Maine, a whisper drifts in from the sea.

Leviathan.

Not a name. Rather, a title. Leviathan is the Woman Eater, the monster who lives beneath the sea, said to have an appetite for disobedient wives, for ungrateful daughters, for women who don't fit neatly into society's boxes.

Leviathan is a punishment.

That's what Marley's banking on.

She stands on the edge of a cliff overlooking the Atlantic, a lighthouse at her back. The cliff isn't high enough for the jump to kill her—at least, she doesn't think so. Still, the blackness down below sends a shiver up her spine. The foam on the waves is the only reason the water level's visible at all.

The September night is cold. Reluctantly, she strips down to her underwear and a t-shirt, shedding her boots, socks, pants, long-sleeved shirt, and sweater and folding them into a pile. She'll leave them as evidence that she was once here, a little reminder that they'll never erase her, not completely.

"Hear me, Leviathan," Marley says, closing her eyes and holding her arms out to her sides, "and answer my plea."

She jumps.

Zola Ward strides purposefully through her precinct. She ignores the whispers of her fellow detectives, whispers that have been following her for six months now, ever since she transferred here. It's not just the fact that she's new. It's that she's new and a woman and black in a state that's ninety-six-percent white and almost as conservative.

Can't beat the views, though.

"Got another one for you," says her sergeant as soon as she sits down.

"Oh, yeah? What is it this time?"

"Missing person." He drops the file on her desk and walks away.

The captain, old-school to the bone, keeps punting her the cases no one else wants—the junkies, the prostitutes, the runaways. The ones that could've been prevented. The ones nobody cares about. And she'll keep taking them because someone's got to look out for the forgotten.

Zola opens the file. The details change, but the song remains the same. Marley Pelletier. Waitress at The Whistlin' Whale, a pub on the outskirts of town. Reported missing by her husband, Mark. Says she had a late shift on Friday night so he went to sleep before she got home, like usual. When he woke up today, there was nothing to suggest she'd been home at all.

After reading through the husband's statement twice, she calls the local hospital, but no one's been brought in in the last sixteen hours that matches Marley's description.

She slides her sweater on and heads out to The Whistlin' Whale, a modest two-story structure, its wooden walls distressed from the salty, damp wind pervasive on the coast. Inside, it's pretty much what Zola expected—plain wooden furniture, drink selection that emphasizes cheap beer, chalk sandwich board proclaiming lobster bisque as the day's special. Saturday afternoon means it's only on the cusp of getting busy, but even with just a quarter of the tables occupied, desperation fills the air.

The desperation of people in a tiny coastal town that offers nothing but the comfort of the known.

It took her a while after she arrived to figure out what it was, but now? Now, she can feel it everywhere she goes.

A middle-aged waitress approaches, with the saggy look that comes from living the same day every day. Her nametag reads 'Jo.' "Sit wherever you'd like, honey. I'll be with you in a minute."

"Oh, I'm not here for a meal," Zola says, flashing her badge. "I'm Detective Ward. I just need a moment of your time, Jo."

Jo shrugs. "In that case, guess you can talk to me on my smoke break."

Zola follows her into the back alley and holds up a photo of Marley. "Do you know this woman?"

Jo curls her shoulders forward as she lights the cigarette dangling from her lips. She leans against the pub's back wall, takes a long drag, and blows out the smoke in a long sigh. "She in trouble?"

"She was reported missing this morning by her husband. She works here, doesn't she?"

Jo stares at the cracked concrete and twists her lips before nodding.

Zola takes her time putting the photo back in her pocket and getting out her notebook and pen. There's something this woman isn't saying. "When was the last time you saw her?"

Jo meets Zola's gaze and says softly, almost pityingly, "You're not going to find her."

No challenge in the words, no bravado. Simple fact.

"What makes you say that?" Zola asks.

"Women like that, with lives like that—they don't want to be found."

Zola furrows her brow. Is Jo intimating that Mark hit his wife? Maybe Mark got out of control, killed Marley by accident, then covered it up. More often than not, a missing-person case has something to do—directly or indirectly—with the spouse.

"She ever say anything about her husband?"

"You're not from around here, are you?"

Zola slips her notepad and pen back into her coat pocket. She won't get any more information from this woman, and unfortunately, what she got already isn't a lot. "I think we're done here."

Jo shakes her head through the haze of smoke. "You've got this look, like you're going to carry the world all by yourself. But, honey, all that will get you is a bad back."

"Thank you for your time," Zola says through a tight jaw.

As she stalks out of the alley, Jo calls, "Check Colossus Cliff. You'll find what you're looking for."

Zola pauses, turns. "How do you know?"

"Dropped her off there last night."

"You dropped her off at the top of a cliff?" Unbelievable. "Did you ever hear her express suicidal thoughts?"

Jo drops her cigarette to the concrete, grounds it out, and strolls closer. "Ever wonder why no one goes to the shore at night? Why the sun goes down and you feel a strange stirring to go inside?

Why you look out at the ocean and instead of feeling awe, you feel uneasy?"

Not this again.

"There's a monster in those waves, Detective," Jo says. "We call her Leviathan."

"I'm not listening to urban legends," Zola says before walking off.

Jo's drawling "See you around, Detective" follows her out of the alley.

On a gloomy, overcast afternoon like this, the park where Colossus Cliff is located isn't crowded. Zola drives slowly up winding lanes barely big enough for one car before emerging from the cover of the trees. She pulls into a small parking lot, only eight or ten spaces, a little ways away from a red and white striped lighthouse.

The air is silent save for the rustle of leaves in the breeze and the constant breaking of the waves. Hands on her hips, she looks out at the ocean. She came to the coast because it's pretty, because it's calming, and pretty and calming mean she won't lost another partner on the job. But this cliff is anything but. Though it looks innocuous, there's an undercurrent of . . . wrongness she can't quite name.

Just the waitress's old urban legend getting to her. She shakes it off.

A hiking trail leads into the woods to her right. Since it'll be the biggest area to search, she saves it for last and heads instead toward the lighthouse. A sign on the door explains it's locked except for special occasions, and there's no sign of broken entry.

A wooden railing sits at the edge of the cliff. It extends from the parking lot past the lighthouse, but not much past it. If Marley had jumped, she wouldn't have had to go over the barrier, just around it. On the hunt for any sign of the missing woman, Zola strides through the ankle-high grass to the railing's end only to be greeted by a neatly folded pile of discarded clothes.

So, Marley's a jumper, after all. Damn.

In a way, it disappoints Zola. She does this job to get the answers, but sometimes, the knowing hurts worse.

She takes a picture of the pile of clothes and pulls on gloves before sifting through it. A sweater, a long-sleeved shirt, socks, boots, and brown pants, nothing in the pockets. Unremarkable except for the fact that they're hanging out on the edge of a cliff overlooking the ocean.

The thing about life this far up the coast is in the autumn, the water's pretty damn cold. If the fall didn't kill or severely injure Marley and she managed to pull herself back to shore, she'd have died of hypothermia in under half an hour.

Damn. This isn't how she wanted this to end.

There's something out there in the water, though. Something that calls to her.

Something she can't ignore.

She calls the find in to the precinct while absentmindedly studying the series of switchbacks off to her left that leads to the rocky shore. When she hangs up, she traipses down the trail. Might as well do a little more investigating before the crime-scene techs get here.

Gray rocks smoothed by the surf make the going uneven but not treacherous. Down here, closer to the sea, the itch, the inkling grows more insistent. She stares out at the water, almost the same dull gray as the rocks it brushes up against.

There's nothing out there. Leviathan is a myth, a legend, something made up to scare her because she's new to town.

Isn't it?

She takes a step closer to the churning water.

She cuts to the right, positioning herself directly below the pile of clothes up on the cliff. Not much land between the craggy cliff face and the water here. Jumping straight into the water would've been easy.

Being pushed into the water would've been easy, too.

A shiver cuts through the air and down her spine, and beneath her sweater, goosebumps rise. Because there it is again.

The call.

This time, she can't push it away.

She walks back to the section of shore that slopes gradually into the ocean and wades in. Her mind is blank save for one thing—an instinctual force driving her home, a home that isn't behind her but before her. Her boots fill with water she knows is ice-cold but instead feels pleasant and welcoming. A few more steps, and her pants are soaked through from the knee down.

She's up to her chest before the land drops off sharply, and she plunges in.

Something solid and warm wraps around her middle, tugging her down, down, down until they come to an abrupt stop. The water's murky. She blinks until her eyes adjust to the darkness.

There's a woman beside her, one arm around Zola's waist. Only she's not a woman. Not *just* a woman. The form is mostly right, except for the webbing between fingers and toes. The naked skin has taken on a blue-green hue and is partially coated in scales. And slits carved into her neck undulate as she breathes.

Gills.

What the hell?

Zola tries to break out of the woman's grasp.

TAKE HER BACK, a voice booms.

Zola stops fighting. She can't tell if the voice is just in her mind or in both their minds or spoken aloud, but she knows what it means.

Leviathan.

Zola follows the woman's gaze into a cave, bioluminescent algae clinging to its ceiling. One by one, shadows resolve into more women, some of whose scales have progressed further than others'. Among the women, Marley, and behind them, a gigantic mass with rippling tentacles.

"Is she not one of us, Mother?" asks the woman holding Zola.

SHE DOES NOT BELONG HERE. NOT YET.

Though the shadowed leader doesn't turn toward her, Zola somehow knows she's being addressed directly when the voice booms, YOU PROTECT THEM ON LAND. YOUR PROTECTION IS NOT NEEDED HERE. YOU MUST RETURN.

Zola opens her mouth to speak, but she cannot speak here, not in this realm.

Water rushes into her mouth, her lungs, and this world under the sea goes black.

Salt water pushes itself out of Zola's lungs and up through her trachea to spill onto the rocks. Violent coughs rack her body until her eyes are leaking tears and her throat feels like it's on fire. Once the water's gone, or almost gone, her stomach clenches again and again until there's nothing left inside.

Finally, chest heaving, she lies on her back. The sky above is gray, just as when she went under. Then two faces lean into her line of sight— EMTs, from the blue of their uniform shirts.

"You see Leviathan out there?" one of them asks with a half-grin as he helps her into a sitting position and gets a blanket around her shoulders.

Leviathan. The one the town calls the Woman Eater. Images flash in her mind. An underwater community—a safe haven?—full of women who used to be human, now living under the protection of their mother.

Not a Woman Eater at all. A Woman Protector.

Zola's teeth chatter as she answers, "No. I didn't see anything."

Zola slides into the back booth in The Whistlin' Whale. She taps her fingers against the tabletop until Jo saunters over, pours steaming water into a mug, and tosses down a tea bag. She offers a knowing smile before she walks away.

Zola sinks into the booth, glad to be done with the week of desk duty the captain assigned her as punishment for investigating the seaside alone, no matter that he hasn't bothered to assign her a partner.

Not that she's ready for that.

Jo returns with a stack of blueberry pancakes and sets the plate down with a clatter. Then she leans against the back of the opposite booth and looks down at Zola. "So? What's the official word on Marley?"

"Probable suicide," Zola says as she unrolls the napkin of silverware.

Of course, the case will remain open until it goes cold, which it will, since they don't have the confirmation of a body. But that's not what Jo's concerned about because it's one thing for a thing to exist and quite another for everyone to know about it.

To know about *her.*

"And what do you think, Detective?" Jo asks.

Zola lifts the bag out of her tea and sets it on the saucer. The water's a perfect golden-brown now, just the way she likes it. "I think . . . some women don't want to be found."

The only people who'll be hearing that particular truth from Zola's lips are the women who need it, the women she's charged to protect.

Jo nods, satisfied with the answer. "Enjoy your meal, honey."

Zola tucks into the pancakes. She will.

How You Find It

You're twelve when the voices start. They come at night, in the darkness, when you're not distracted with school and homework and softball. You'll learn later that when the sky gets darker, the veil between this world and whatever's out there gets thinner. It's easier on both of you.

You're twelve, and you can't sleep—you *won't* sleep—because you need to listen. That's all you can do, and sometimes, it's all people need. But because you're not sleeping well, everyone—your mom and dad, your older brother who protects you even when his friends call you annoying— thinks you're having the same nightmares you did when you were seven, the ones where clowns had skeleton bodies and pet skeleton scorpions. That's not it at all, but you don't know how to explain what it is, so you let them drag you to a therapist.

She's kind, at least. That was your one criterion, so your dad got this lady's name from the army veteran across the street, and here you are. In an office full of bursts of color. Toys on the windowsill. A bright blue couch. A painting hanging above it that's just rainbow splashes on canvas. It almost makes your eyes hurt, but it does lighten the confusion you carry in your chest, calms you just a touch.

You don't care to remember her name. Your parents, occasionally Jack, will drive you here each week, and there are much more important names you need to remember. You need to save brain space for those.

She's kind, but sometimes she doesn't make sense. A few weeks in, she says, "Pain is energy, and energy needs somewhere to go. Do you understand?"

You shake your head. You're twelve. You haven't gotten to physics yet in science class.

"Find an outlet," she says. "You can't bottle this all up inside. It needs somewhere to go." She leans forward, an expectant smile gracing her pretty face. "Do you like art class?"

You nod. You like that she lets you respond nonverbally instead of badgering you to talk more, like all the other adults in your life.

"What do you like to do in art class?" she asks.

You pull a sketchpad out of your book bag, slumped at your feet, and open it to a page of a lion eating the stars.

"You like to draw?" she asks.
You nod again. You love to draw.
"Good," she says. "Use that."
And you do.

You're seventeen and still seeing your therapist—her name's Kate Lansing—when she gives you the idea. You've gone through so many sketchbooks they take up a whole shelf on your bookcase. Your mom's been begging you to throw them out, and when you bring this to Kate, she suggests starting a blog.

All they want is to be listened to. One by one, you scan each page in your sketchbooks, write out these stories, and post them on a blog you've called Whisperings. Every day, a new face, a new story.

The blog occupies a little corner of the internet, not bothering anyone, and no one bothers it. Despite its anonymity, or perhaps because of it, it serves its purpose well—gives you an outlet, gives these people voices that everyone can hear, not just you. It's the steadiest thing in your life.

Until one day.

One day, when you're twenty-one and living in a campus efficiency and subsisting on microwavable dollar noodles, your laptop chimes with an incoming message, the only message your blog has ever received.

From KaleidoscopeRainyDays:

Why are you drawing my sister?

Six words. Six words that shake you to the core. Because these people whose stories you've listened to, these people you've drawn, are people who have died alone, died unloved. They've been wronged, a good percentage of them have been murdered, but no one's ever stepped forward to claim them.

And now, even though it's online and you can't quite tell the tone, you know you've caused this KaleidoscopeRainyDays, whoever they are, pain. That's the last thing you want, which means you have to make it right.

The cursor blinks at you, accusing. But you don't know what to say. You don't know what to say to make it right.

This KaleidoscopeRainyDays's sister, the subject of your last post, she got murdered in an alley behind a dive bar near the back entrance of her apartment. A dive bar and an apartment complex that are just across town. If she was local, maybe the sibling is, too.

With a deep breath, you straighten your shoulders and set fingers to the keyboard.

I can explain. Will you meet me?

The coffee shop KaleidoscopeRainyDays picks is on campus.

You hadn't expected them to live so close. Maybe you've passed them on the way to class countless times. Maybe they're in your major, in some of your classes. Maybe they work in the campus post-office and have handed you packages. Or at the library and have checked books out to you. It makes you shudder despite not having that reaction in the aspect of your life that should induce it.

You shake that thought away and settle into a table at the back of the shop, situate yourself so you can keep an eye on the front door—without taking your coat off because you haven't yet cast off the chill of the day. You've ordered a London fog, and you curl your hands around the cup for warmth.

When a few minutes pass without any sign of the sibling, you slip a sketchbook from your bag and open it to a fresh page. This is the only thing that makes sense. Pencil across the page, graphite on cream. When your hands are moving, fingers gripping pencil firmly but not tightly, streaks of gray turning into a picture beneath your skilled hand—that's when life falls into place. It's not about getting teased for being weird. It's not about always feeling alone. It's not about hearing voices belonging to those who have died with pain or anger or without dignity.

It's about creation. It's all about creation. Keep going forward, blazing a trail. Keep smiling, touching others' lives. Keep drawing, lighting the darkness. Create, create, create until your very movement, your very thought, your very life—all acts of creation.

A throat clearing. Then a strong, soft voice saying, "Are you the one from that blog? The one who drew the picture of my sister?"

You look up into muted brown eyes and a face that's striking even though the woman in front of you isn't smiling. For some reason, you expected a brother.

The sister lifts her eyebrows at you. She asked you a question and, like most normal people, expects a response.

"Um, yes," you say, standing and reaching out your hand. "That's me."

She doesn't shake it.

"Right." You wipe your palms on the thighs of your jeans and sit down again. "Can I buy you a cup of tea?"

"No."

Okay. This isn't how you expected this to go. You'd expected curiosity, not open hostility. Time to readjust. Or at least try to. You don't spend much time around other people, so . . . You take a sip of your tea, lick your lips, frown.

The woman takes the seat across from you. "How did you know that stuff about my sister?"

You spin the cup of tea between your fingers. "I . . . talked to her."

"She never mentioned you."

"No, that's not really what I mean."

"What do you mean, then?" She leans forward. "Because I don't like judging people, but I can tell you're a creep. And if you don't tell me what you want from me and what you wanted from my sister, I'm going to call the police. And I've got them on speed-dial because that's what happens when your sister gets murdered. You got a detective on speed-dial in case you run into a creeper like you."

"I'm not a creeper," you say and immediately put a hand in front of your mouth because that's exactly what creepers say.

"Oh, you're not, are you?"

You lower your hand. "I just want to help."

"And how is drawing murdered people and putting those drawings up online and telling the world how they died helping?"

"They're not all murder victims," you say. Then you squeeze your eyes shut because that's not the point. "It's just . . . There are so many people out there—" Women, mostly. "—who don't have voices, especially after they've . . . Well, I didn't mean to hurt anyone. My only intention was to keep them from being silenced."

She lets out a heavy sigh. "Intentions don't matter when people get hurt."

You nod. "And I hurt you, and I'm sorry about that. I can take down the post."

"Good."

With a deep breath, you make an effort to still your fidgeting hands. You'd thought this was about KaleidoscopeRainyDays, about finding closure, so you assumed she'd do the talking. But she isn't. She's staring at you with hard eyes that, in sunlight and in happiness, would be so, so soft.

She's not speaking, and there's so much to say, so your blurt out one of those things. "They can't tie him to the scene, can they?"

Her lip curls in a snarl, and her voice is deadly low when she asks, "How did you know that?" When you don't answer right away, she barks, "How?"

"I talked to her," you say again, this time adding, "after she died."

Scoffing, she rolls her eyes in frustration and stands. "I should've known. I should've known," she breathes. Louder, she says, "So, you're not a creep, but you're the weirdo who, what? Thinks she hears dead people?"

"I'm not asking you to believe me."

"No? This is how you get attention, though, isn't it? Telling outlandish stories? Backing them up with info you probably get hacking into the local police station from your basement?"

You reel back at her words, at the accusation in them. You don't do this for attention. You've never wanted that. In fact, attention gives you hives. You do it because there's no other way to calm the voices and because the people who speak to you are people who *need* a voice and you can give that to them.

"You may think you're trying to help, but this doesn't help anyone," she says, quiet and angry, before stomping off.

"W-wait. The phone— The phone's in the grate! Check the—"

The bell above the door jingles as she walks out.

Well.

You sit back down and stare at your tea. You slide your fingers around the mug for warmth.

At least you didn't take off your coat.

You sit on Kate's couch with your face between your knees. You can't see her expression, but she's smiling at you. She's always smiling at you. She says you're endearing. You never believe it, but she keeps saying it.

"What do you think you could've done differently?" she asks gently.

Been normal. Been less weird. Been reassuring instead of just creepy.

You shrug as best you can in the position and mumble into your knees, "I don't know."

"You don't have any control over how other people react."

"I know."

"You know in the sense that you can parrot it back to me, but you don't believe it, not really."

You want to. It's just that you feel like you missed something. The sensation's been following you around for days now.

Kate says your name gently.

You never even learned her real name. Maybe that's what's bothering you.

You sit up, take a giant breath.

Kate smiles at you, like always. "Well? Do you believe it?"

"I'll work on it."

"That's good enough for me."

It's after two AM when a knock sounds at your door. You're awake—you've never gotten out of the night-owl habit—but definitely not in the mood for company, especially considering you just took mac and cheese off the stove. You're never in the mood for company. It's not like you have friends to expect. You exchange your bowl for the softball bat you keep in the entranceway and peek through the keyhole.

KaleidoscopeRainyDays, leaning against the opposite wall, head tipped back.

Is she . . . Is she sleeping? Did she fall asleep against the wall?

You unlock the door and open it. "Hello? Kaleidoscope? Are you okay?"

She straightens up. Her face is streaked with tears, and her eyes have that heavy, slack look that comes with alcohol consumption. She braces one hand on the wall behind her. "My sister died."

"Yeah, she did," you say softly.

"My sister was murdered."

"Yeah, she was."

"And they didn't catch the guy because of a lack of evidence."

"No, they didn't."

She pauses, hitches in a breath, frowns at her own hands like they're the ones responsible for the murder of her sister. "I told the police what you said. I told them about the grate."

You wait. What she's saying is for herself, not for you.

"They found her phone. They found her phone, and they found blood that isn't hers under the case. It's his. I know it is. They'll get him now. They have to."

"I'm glad," you say. He deserves to get caught. Not all of the ones who deserve it actually get caught, but it settles a piece of your heart back into place when it does happen, and you hope it'll happen in this case.

Her face falls into her hands as a sob shakes her frame.

You swallow hard.

She's drunk, and she's crying, and you're totally unprepared to deal with either of those things. There are reasons you live alone. This is one of them.

She's hurting, though, and you sort of know how to deal with that. You know how to make hot chocolate and how to wrap her in a soft blanket and how to sit her down on the couch and how to wait for her to speak instead of forcing words out of her.

You know how to do these things, so you invite her in, and, surprisingly, she says yes.

She calls your name.

You sip the last of your tea and set the mug in the sink. You'll wash it in the morning. You pad back into the bedroom. Your latest sketchpad, already half full, sits on your bed stand, you update the blog almost every week, and you still talk with Kate. But you're learning. You talk more, smile more. You go outside more, enjoy the sunshine more.

You climb into bed, and she immediately curls her arms around you and presses a sleepy kiss to the side of your neck. There is peace in this small apartment, under these sheets, beneath the ceiling fan that turns lazily above you. Here is the truth you have learned—peace is neither big nor grand. Sometimes, it's simply two people full of sorrow and wonder and hope who find comfort in one another.

You breathe in deep, inhale her scent that's in your clothes, your sheets. In response, she squeezes your middle. Briefly. To let you know she's there.

You don't need her to believe you, but she does, and that makes all the difference in the world.

Blood of the Covenant

Nevenka craned her neck toward the palace of the gods, which disappeared into the clouds so only the foundation, carved from pure white stone, was visible. The climb through the forest blanketing the mountainside would be hard but not impossible. Not impossible because Nevenka's benefactor had supplied her well and because the forest wasn't meant to serve as a barrier. The gods were forbidden from coming down.

The four prototypic gods—the Old Watch—had self-exiled themselves in a covenant with the seven gods of the New Watch, a covenant that had left the Godless Lands between their territories. So no, the gods couldn't come down.

But that didn't mean a human couldn't go up.

So Nev did.

Her most useful assets were her skinny frame and her speed. She wasn't built for fighting, and, indeed, she'd lost the majority of street fights she'd found her way into. But growing up in the gutters had taught her survival, and survival had taught her stealth.

A pity she didn't actually need it.

The palace was vast—and empty—with open corridors supported by white columns that reflected the moonlight. She'd never stopped to consider how the gods lived way up here. She'd barely considered the gods at all, not until she'd stumbled into one's temple—quite by accident—all those months ago. Now, she recalled no stories of the gods engaging mortals to cater to their whims or fashioning themselves servants out of clay or something.

It was so quiet that Nev almost didn't dare breathe for fear of ruining the death-like veil that had fallen over the place.

Fallen . . . or had been thrown?

Were the gods not gods at all but ghosts?

Nev had to get what she came for and get out as quickly as possible. Swallowing the fear that clawed at her skin, she crept deeper into the palace, full of shadows.

At each intersection, she paused to listen for footsteps; at each open door, conversation or movement from within. She made it almost to the center of the palace before she encountered life— two women conversing across a dining table. Even in profile, they were recognizable as Enid, the god of Life, and Morgan, the god of Death. As Nev had traveled through the Old Watch territories on her way here, those faces had been etched into countless statues, painted onto countless temple walls.

Nev moved on. If this were simply the dwelling of a rich merchant or suchlike, she'd know exactly where to find their valuables. Most people were predictable like that when it came to greed.

This was the home of gods, though, and what she sought wasn't the type of prize that would interest mortals.

Perhaps it shouldn't have come as a surprise, then, that she located it in a modest room tucked away in a seemingly forgotten corner of the palace. The walls here were made from rich dark wood, a plain, soft rug covered the floor, and the only furniture was two cushioned chairs and a sofa.

In the center of the room was a glass case set upon a stand. Light emanated from within, though Nevenka couldn't divine the source. Magic, most like.

Inside the case were four pieces of a medallion. The medallion, which would have been the size of a dinner plate had all eleven pieces been present, was the marker of the covenant between the gods of the Old Watch and of the New. A covenant that could be broken only when the medallion was restored to its original whole state.

Nev's entire body vibrated with her deep breath. It couldn't be this simple. Surely, even deities who lived among the clouds would more fiercely protect objects of such magnitude.

Behind her, someone gasped. Nev turned just as a glass of wine fell to the floor at the stranger's feet.

Only it was no stranger. The petite stature, the brown skin, the curls framing the face, the piercing brown eyes—all unmistakable.

Freya, the god of love.

"What are you doing here?" Freya asked breathlessly. "Who are you?"

When Nev had glimpsed Morgan and Enid, they had been at the opposite end of the hall. Here, an actual god stood not ten paces away, close enough to see every detail on her face, stunning not only for its beauty but also for its kindness.

She shook herself out of her paralysis and dropped to her knees. "Forgive me, Mighty Freya, for trespassing into your home."

"What is your name?"

"Nevenka, Lady."

"Stand, Nevenka."

Nev did so but kept her head bent and her gaze on the rug where the wine had soaked in. Would Freya guess her purpose here? If so, how bad would the punishment be? The longer the god studied her in silence, the more wildly Nev's heart beat. Could a mortal die simply from being looked at by a god? Because Nev, her skin tingling and her heart thudding against her ribs, felt close.

"Why are you here?" Freya asked, less harshly than expected. But when Nev opened her mouth to reply, Freya said, "And don't lie to me. Even the patron of love has little patience for liars . . . or thieves."

Nev's gaze snapped up only to be caught by Freya's.

Freya's expression fell somewhere between a smirk and a grimace. "We gods may not have had contact with mortals for over two centuries, but I know a thief when I see one. Now tell me your purpose."

Nev's benefactor couldn't help her here. She could rely only on herself. It was unwise to lie to a god, and it was especially unwise to lie directly to a god's face. Nev would rather get the punishment over with instead of dragging this out. It wasn't as if the outcome mattered at all. If she failed, another would be sent in her place. There was no stopping this. There was only delay. There was only hoping to get through as unscathed as possible.

"Leva sent me," said Nev, "to steal your pieces of the covenant medallion."

Freya, with a sharp exhalation and a palm over her heart, sank to the couch, a reaction far from the fury Nev had anticipated.

"I knew it," Freya murmured to herself. That Nevenka overheard seemed inconsequential. "I knew she would start this one day. I just didn't think it would be so soon."

So soon? The war between the gods had happened over two hundred years ago. Then again, time moved differently for immortals.

Nev, having grown up on the streets, wasn't stupid. She knew she was Leva's pawn. She simply hadn't stopped to consider how her actions would affect anyone but herself. Now, for the first time, she did. If Leva possessing the medallion meant the gods would go to war again, they might scorch the whole earth. And what good would it be to never go hungry again if there was no world to be hungry in?

Freya, staring at the empty hearth, worried her lip with her hand, almost like she'd forgotten Nev was there. If the medallion was as precious as Leva led her to believe, why wasn't Freya scolding or striking or even killing her?

"You aren't . . . You aren't going to stop me?" Nev asked.

Freya finally looked up once more. "Do you want me to?"

What sort of question was that? "I . . . I don't know."

"No, of course you don't. How many summers have you seen? Fourteen?"

Nev straightened. "Fifteen." She wasn't *that* small.

"Right," Freya said with a condescending smile. "Fifteen. You don't know. Why would you?"

Know what? Nev wanted to ask. But for the first time in her life, she kept her mouth shut.

When she got through this—*if* she got through it—she'd pray every day to every god whose name she knew that she'd never have to speak face-to-face with one of them ever again.

If conversation this confounding was what awaited them, no wonder humans never came up the mountain.

"Sit, Thief," said Freya, lifting an elegant arm to indicate the chair across from her.

Nev sat, though she couldn't take pleasure in the soft cushions or the luxurious upholstery.

"Do you know," Freya said, "how the other gods came to be?"

Nev shook her head. Street rats didn't have the opportunity to pay much attention to religion, and religion never paid much attention to them.

"We created them, called them our daughters," Freya said, "but what did we know of mothering?"

Nev sank back in her chair. Weren't the gods as mothers to all mortals? Or at least meant to be?

"Over time," Freya continued, "they learned what all children learn—that parents, even immortal ones, are far from faultless. Six learned to accept that. One could not."

The god's pained expression tugged at Nev's conscience until something she'd said tugged at her curiosity. "Why seven?" An unlucky number in their world. Perhaps this conflict between the gods was the root of that unluckiness.

"We agreed that each would create two daughters," Freya said. "We ourselves had grown weary with our duties to the mortal world, and so we decided the duties of each pair would be complementary. We sought, as parents do, to make life easier for them."

Nev's stomach sunk. She should have asked more questions at the outset, but would Leva have even told her? Instead, Nev had been too concerned with the promise of stability, of never going hungry again, of always having a roof over her head. She pushed away the trepidation that memory dredged up. "What happened?"

Freya's gaze was faraway when she said, "One among us went back on that agreement. One among us gave life to only one."

"Leva." Of course. Nev willed Freya to meet her gaze. "But who? Who was her mother?"

Freya folded her hands in front of her and stared out the window as the trespasser left, her footsteps silent against the stone. She had let the girl take the medallion pieces not because she didn't care but because she knew Leva would never stop. This enmity between them must run its course.

And she must warn the others.

She would tell Aeron first, though. The god of war deserved that much.

Freya found her in her library, where the dark shelves and furniture contrasted with Aeron's golden hair. Behind her desk, she sat stiffly, despite not having worn her armor for centuries.

She would need it soon, Freya realized with a pang, much sooner than she knew.

At her entrance, Aeron looked up from a book, and her expression softened as it only did around Freya, who couldn't bring herself to return the smile.

"What's wrong?" Aeron asked, concern in her eyes, as she rose.

"Something has happened," Freya said, "and something will happen, and I'm afraid."

With gentle hands, Aeron led her to a sofa, where they sat together. "Tell me."

Freya did, for they kept no secrets. Unsurprisingly, Aeron had suspected nothing. How like the god of war to have created a child whose loneliness would serve as justification for devastating the earth. How even more like the god of war not to have predicted it, not to have listened to Freya's counsel.

And how like the god of love to care blindly for such a woman.

Aeron went to stand by a window, hands behind her back as she gazed out at the dark clouds surrounding them.

A millennium they had lived and loved, and yet Freya would never truly understand what went on in Aeron's mind. She'd spend a thousand millennia learning if only Aeron—and Leva— would let her.

Freya joined her at the window and tried unsuccessfully to catch her gaze. "Do you not see how dangerous this could be? For all of us?"

"She's a child. She poses no true threat."

"She is a god. Of course she is a threat," Freya said, fury leaking into her voice.

Aeron turned then, her expression betraying her surprise. She had no concern for her own life, her own safety, but Freya—no, Freya could not bear it if anything were to happen at Leva's hands.

"You made her the Carrier of Hearts, and you made no other to help her bear that burden," Freya said more calmly. "She is strong, but she is not you. And you're her mother. You must be the one to confront her before this can go any further."

"And how am I meant to do that? I cannot leave this palace, Freya. None of us can. And Leva cannot come here."

"She can with the medallion. It will take the girl some time to reach the territories of the New Watch, but Leva will come, and we must prepare."

The intensity of Aeron's blue eyes, normally so warm, made Freya take a step back.

"Then I'll call my warriors," said Aeron. "I'll be ready."

"Not everything between you two needs to be battle and bloodshed."

"What would you have me do?"

"Love her!"

Aeron dropped her gaze as the silence shuttered between them. Freya reached out, always ready to soothe, to calm, but Aeron pulled away.

When Aeron finally spoke, her voice was low. "I'm not like you, Freya. If I couldn't love her to her satisfaction before, why would I be able to now?"

The confession cracked Freya's heart. "You're not incapable of love. No one is incapable of love."

Not even the god of war.

If only Aeron herself believed that.

Nevenka paused over the threshold of Leva's temple. The medallion pieces, in a pouch at her hip, weighed her down. The trip to the New Watch's territories had given her ample time to think, and she was still as confused as ever. Freya had let her go, had practically given her blessing. Did that mean this was the part she was destined to play? Could she turn around, turn away from Leva forever, and never look back?

If she did that, though, she'd still be wet in the rainy season and cold in winter and hungry all the time. In the end, what did it matter which gods ruled which lands?

It didn't matter to her at all. She was too inconsequential for the gods to care. This way, at least, she wouldn't have to worry about surviving.

She stepped into the temple.

Leva, tall and imposing, waited for her by the altar, her frame backlit by the afternoon sun through the window. She looked different than the last time they'd met. Leather pauldrons encased her broad shoulders, a cape flowed behind her, and a sword hung at her hip. Though Nev had only ever seen representations of Aeron, the influence was apparent. The Carrier of Hearts was become the Daughter of War.

In homage or in mockery?

"Do you have what I sent you for?"

Leva's booming voice dragged Nev forward. At the foot of the altar, she dropped to a knee. She had made her choice. There could be no second thoughts now.

With trembling fingers, she untied the pouch from her belt and offered it up in cupped palms.

Leva snatched it and stepped around to the altar, upon which lay a gold chalice and the remaining seven pieces of the medallion. Had her sisters given them up willingly, or had they been pawns, too? Gently, almost reverently, she slid the last four from the pouch and aligned them in a circle, a thin space separating each piece. All she needed to do was connect them. And what then?

Nev scrambled to her feet to watch.

Leva's chest heaved as she pushed the pieces together. Cracks of light emanated from each juncture, so bright Nev threw her arm over her eyes even though she couldn't look away. Leva held the medallion above the cup, the light fading until it winked out. The gold of the medallion melted into red, and then the medallion itself liquefied and drained into the cup.

"Is that . . . ?" Nev asked, breathless.

Leva's gaze flicked dismissively toward Nev. "Blood? Yes, the blood with which we forged the covenant."

Nev's stomach roiled. "All this to wreak revenge on your mother?"

"Vengeance is a small, human desire," Leva said. Her cold, penetrating gaze sent a chill through Nev. "You cannot understand what I seek, so do not try." Then, with bloody hands, she lifted the cup to her lips and drank.

Eyes closed, she set the empty chalice on the altar. In the next heartbeat, everything changed, and yet nothing did. There was no outward sign, but Nev felt it in her bones. She had unleashed a dreadful, immeasurable force upon the earth, and there was no going back.

Leva opened her eyes, spread her arms, and breathed in, seeming to inhale power as well as air. "Thank you for your service, Nevenka. I will see that you are well compensated."

She strode past a quaking Nev and paused in the threshold of the temple. Turning just enough to show her profile, she said, "Retribution implies the end. This is only the beginning."

She walked away, stepping foot on solid land for the first time in two hundred years.

Nev shrank back against a pillar.

By the gods . . . What had she done?

Lonesome

The log split as Ryn drove her axe through it. She was halfway through her work for the day when the sun peeked over the horizon to light the homestead in pinkish gray. Sleep rarely came easily, and when it did, it came accompanied by nightmares even worse than the memories. The work cleared her head, and the dark didn't bother her, not with her elven vision.

Legally, the land encompassing her homestead and Lonesome, the town nestled in the valley below, belonged to neither humans nor elves, both of whom acted like the war still raged. As long as it stayed far away from her land, Ryn didn't much care.

Even in the dawn chill, sweat soaked her shirt and the brim of her hat. She welcomed the ache in her shoulders from chopping wood. She welcomed any discomfort that took her mind from the constant twinge in her left hand, an unfortunate souvenir of her service in the war. She rubbed idly at the scar tissue on her palm as she paused to watch the sunrise paint the sky orange. Another day about to begin. Another day that would inevitably be just like all the days that had come before. In her darkest moments, she wished she could trade the dullness and emptiness of this life for the horrors she experienced in the war.

That was why she had to work to keep her body busy and keep her mind from that dark place. She stacked the last of the wood and headed to the barn to feed the pegasi, calygreyhounds, and unicorns. The animals she stabled, fewer than a dozen in all, had been used as mounts by the elven army until injuries rendered them of no further use. She was a lot like them, she supposed.

Ryn dumped feed into each of their troughs and opened the stall doors. Once the creatures were through with their meal, they'd meander into the pasture to laze in the sun.

She traipsed back to the farmhouse, where Humphrey greeted her at the door. He was a small thing, as all his species were, about the size of her forearm and agile enough to crawl all over her when he was excited. His deep blue scales shimmered in the early sunlight as he scuttled up her leg and torso to perch on her shoulder.

"Hey, boy," she said, giving him a scratch. Her voice was rough with disuse.

He leaned into her touch, eyes closing in satisfaction. Unlike her, he usually slept through the night. She cooked breakfast, scrambled eggs and toast with jam, and sat down at the wobbly kitchen table she hadn't been bothered to fix. Humphrey didn't care, either. He leapt from her shoulder to the table surface to gulp down a torn-off hunk of bread.

That was when Ryn heard it—the gallop of horse hooves approaching.

"Stay here," she said to Humphrey. Then she grabbed her rifle from the corner, stormed out of the front door, and aimed it in the direction of town.

The clop-clop-clop grew louder. Her trigger finger twitched, and her heart beat wildly, but she took a slow, steady breath to calm it.

As the horse and its rider galloped around a bend in the path, Ryn let the rifle barrel drop halfway. The rider was human, female, with pale skin and long blonde hair that streamed behind her. The tavern owner. Etta or Hattie or something like that. What the hell was she doing here?

More curious than wary, Ryn hopped down the porch steps. When the horse reached her, the rider slid down from the saddle.

"Please. You have to help me," said the woman, out of breath. Frantic to get her point across, she spoke in a rush. "I didn't know who else to turn to. But you're you, and you're rather broody and frightening up here on the hill all alone, and you're an elf, so you might know where the hell they've taken her."

Ryn slung the rifle over her shoulder. "Taken who? And who's taken them?"

Lonesome saw its share of crime, but it tended toward public drunkenness and petty theft, not kidnapping.

The woman swiped a hand through hair blown wild by the wind. She could barely speak, but Ryn suspected it was from hysteria rather than physical exertion.

Ryn held out her hands, careful not to touch the human. They were sensitive like that. "Take a breath. Take a breath," she said soothingly.

The woman did as Ryn said.

When her breathing had almost returned to normal, Ryn said, "Now, tell me what happened and why you need my help." She'd picked up that much in the woman's flurry of words. The part that stumped her was why any townsperson would seek her out. She came into town once a week or so for supplies and a drink, and yes, she knew the tavern owner by sight, but friends weren't her strong suit.

"They took Gwyn."

"Gwyn, that's . . ."

"She's my sister."

"Oh." Ryn's eyebrows rose in surprise. She was terrible at estimating humans' ages, and so she'd assumed the brood that hung around the tavern and spilled out of its too-small living space on the second floor were the woman's children.

Which one was Gwyn? "You said they took her. Who? And why?"

"Elves," the woman said, meeting Ryn's gaze. "They took her because she's one of them. Her full name's Gwyndarian."

Ryn narrowed her eyes. There was an elf, a girl, in the tavern brood. The few times she'd ventured into the establishment, Ryn had always pretended not to notice, had not wanted the memories the girl raked up, however unintentionally.

She took a step back. "And why me? What am I supposed to do about it?"

The woman gestured at Ryn's ears. "You're an elf. You know what they'd do. You might know where they took her. You could get her back."

"We aren't all the same. Unless you have something to identify who, exactly, took her, there's no hope."

A determined gleam appeared in the woman's eye, and she reached for Ryn's left hand. Ryn jerked it away, grimaced when her nerves ignited with pain. She let out a slow breath as the flare subsided.

"Sorry," the woman said. "I only wanted to show that she's . . . She's like you."

That could mean only one thing, but Ryn didn't believe it. She didn't want to believe it. Mages, even elf mages, were rare, so rare they were valuable, and valuable meant they were used up much too soon. Poor girl.

Her decision wasn't a decision at all.

"Wait in the tavern for me," Ryn said. "If I'm not back in three days' time, well, I won't be coming back at all. And I'll need your horse."

"I have another back at the tavern."

Ryn was already marching back into the farmhouse to gather preparations, so she didn't quite see where the woman was going. "I'll just need the one."

"No, I'm coming with you."

Ryn stopped and turned on the porch. "It's too dangerous for a human."

"She's my sister."

"She's not even blood-related to you."

"It doesn't matter. I'm not going to leave her."

"Who's going to look after the others?"

"Alice is thirteen. She can take care of them while we're gone."

Ryn took her hat off to wipe the sweat from her brow. She squinted into the rising sun. "Fine. But follow my lead." She jerked her chin toward town. "Ready a horse for me. I'll meet you at the tavern as soon as I can."

"It'll be faster if I wait for you and we ride together."

Ryn conceded with a nod. Inside, she grabbed two rucksacks, tossed one to the woman, and gestured to the kitchen. "Here. Fill this with food."

The woman gripped the sack but didn't turn. "My name's Nettie, by the way."

Ryn paused. She'd never been one to adhere to humans' social customs. Or even particularly pay attention to them. "Nettie. You can call me Ryn."

At the noise of their entrance, Humphrey scurried out of the kitchen and blinked up at Nettie.

"And that's Humphrey," Ryn said. She filled her own sack with weapons and ammunition. If they were going where she thought they were going, they'd need them—along with a hefty dose of luck.

Sweat soaked through the underarms and collar of Ryn's shirt as they rode the horses hard. Humphrey had refused to be left behind, and so he'd curled up in her side satchel, out of the wind and sun. Her rifle was tucked into a saddle scabbard, two revolvers rested in belt holsters, and a knife stuck in her right boot. Without her magic, human weapons were her best chance at getting Gwyn back.

At surviving.

The land stretched before them—scrubby grass, red mesas, snow-capped mountains in the distance. Even in this situation, she couldn't be out in the midst of it and not feel some sense of awe. If she was going to die, at least it'd be under the wide open sky.

They set up camp for the night in the shadow of a mesa, out of sight of Elvasia, a prominent town in the elven territories. It was the town Ryn had spent much of her adulthood in, the town that held so much darkness.

Ryn got a modest fire going and Humphrey scuttled around the sand as Nettie unwrapped their cheese, bread, and dried meat. Ryn thanked Nettie as she handed over a bandana full of food and then sat back to contemplate her companion. Although unused to hard riding and surely stiff with it, she hadn't complained once. The harshness of the terrain out here had made even Ryn, who was more accustomed to it, want to complain, but she'd bitten her tongue.

Between bites, Nettie said, "We haven't discussed payment."

"No need," Ryn said gruffly. She wouldn't take it. Not for this job. To stop any protests from Nettie, she gestured to the revolvers strapped to her belt. "You know how to handle those?"

"If I didn't, I wouldn't be alive."

"Good." They were going to need that skill, that spark. Ryn could do a lot of things alone, but knowing what she knew about what was coming, this wouldn't be one of them. "And a rifle?"

"Yep."

Ryn tore off a hunk of bread and chewed as she dug through her rucksack. In the bottom was a box of bullets, the tips tinged with a toxin that interacted with elven blood. It wouldn't kill them, not if it was treated within a few hours, but it was mighty painful. She loaded her rifle with them and then handed them to Nettie so she could load hers, too.

"Where'd you get these?" Nettie asked, and from her tone, it was clear she recognize them.

Ryn didn't look up. "I procured them in case of emergencies."

Nettie shivered, but she loaded the gun and said, "So, what's the plan for the morning?"

Ryn rested her forearms on her thighs. "You'll go into town alone. Ask the first person you come across for Lysyx. Tell them Aerynarya Niavyn sent you. Tell them to send Lysyx out here and only Lysyx."

"And then what?"

Ryn stared hard at the fire. "And then we'll resolve this as peacefully as she lets us." She rolled out her blanket, took off her hat, and lay down. The night was clear, and the stars above burned brightly. That was Ryn's favorite thing about living out here. With a sky like that, she could never quite feel alone.

"What happened?" Nettie asked quietly. "To your hand, I mean."

Most people were too afraid to ask. "Took a bullet. Close range." Not the full story, of course. She massaged her palm, and because she'd grown up to believe you didn't give answers without getting any in return, she asked, "What happened to your parents?" All she knew was they'd left Nettie the tavern shortly after Ryn had arrived in Lonesome. "Elves?"

After a long moment, Nettie quietly said, "Humans." Then she turned her back to Ryn and made clear the conversation was over.

After a sparse breakfast, Nettie rode into town, and Ryn stayed behind in the shadow of the mesa. She fed and watered her horse before sitting down to wait on Lysyx's arrival. But waiting didn't suit her, not when the moment was so close. She checked that her guns were cleaned and loaded, checked that the knife slid easily from her boot. Somehow, though, she sensed this wouldn't come down to bullets from a distance. Something so personal couldn't.

Unmoving as a statue, Humphrey on her shoulder, she stared into the distance until Nettie returned and informed her the gang leader was on her way and, like Ryn suspected, she wasn't coming alone.

Nettie took up her rifle and a position in the shadows. "I could just shoot them all," she suggested grimly. "Only once you get Gwyn's location, of course."

"Everyone's fair game 'cept Lysyx herself. She's mine."

Nettie gave a nod.

When Lysyx and her people approached, Ryn clambered down the hill leading from the mesa and onto the flat land and stopped twenty paces away.

Lysyx dropped off her horse, but the other four—all faces Ryn recognized, Ryn had once commanded—stayed mounted. She rested her right hand on the revolver at her hip.

"Well, well, well, if it isn't Aerynarya Niavyn," Lysyx drawled. "Never thought you'd show your face around here again." Smirking, she jutted her chin at Ryn's belt. "Resorting to guns now? How the mighty have fallen."

"Call off your goons," Ryn said.

"Goons? We were your friends once, Ryn."

"Don't call me that."

One of Lysyx's goons, Vyran, said, "Leave her to me, boss."

Before he could get his leg over the saddle, though, a shot rang out. The bullet impacted his shoulder, and he toppled off his horse with a grunt of pain.

A shadow crossed Lysyx's face. She had obviously forgotten about Nettie, had obviously written her off as just a messenger, just a lowly human.

Ryn sucked in a breath of surprise. Then she said, "Better get him to the physician soon. I hear those bullets do a real number on an elf."

Lysyx held her stare for a moment before gesturing to the others. They gathered up their fallen companion and headed back to town, leaving only Lysyx and Ryn.

And Nettie up in the shade of the mesa. Ryn's chest felt tight. Alone for so long, she'd forgotten what it felt like to be able to rely on someone to have her back.

"I'm here for the girl you took," she said.

Lysyx laughed. "We took a lot more than that from you in the past. Yet you never sought revenge. Why now? What is she to you?"

She's me, Ryn thought. Only with a sister who loved her enough to risk her own life, not a family who spat her out when they were done with her.

"She's no one to me," Ryn said, left hand twinging with pain. The relentless sun beat down on them, and sweat beaded uncomfortably on her neck.

"Then why come for her?"

"Because I was hired, and because she doesn't belong to you."

"I don't answer to you, Ryn."

"You never did," Ryn said. She stared hard at Lysyx so she didn't miss the twitch of her lip or the slight furrow in her brow. "Did you? Tell me—were you plotting your coup your very first night with us?"

"You'd like to think that, wouldn't you? Like to think I was a bad seed from the get-go. Like to think you had nothing to do with my betrayal, with your own downfall." Lysyx shook her head like she was disappointed. "You always were a sentimental fool. It's why you're here now, risking your life for a girl you don't even know."

"What do you want with her? To turn her into a weapon?" Ryn asked. But she thought she knew. Lysyx must have taken Gwyn because she was an elf mage. And Lysyx would still need elf mages because . . . "Because the war isn't over in your mind. Is that it?"

For Lysyx, it would never be over. She was the kind of person whose rage overruled her sense.

There was no other way for that to end but violently.

"You're tiresome, Ryn. Always have been." Lysyx put her hands on her hips. "What's your game here, then? I pull a weapon, and your friend up there shoots me? I don't think so."

"I have no desire to kill you. Just let me have the girl, and I'll be on my way."

Lysyx's eyes were cold, unfeeling. Ryn wondered how she'd never seen it before.

Lysyx rolled up her sleeves. "Then we'll settle this as we used to. No weapons, just fists. Whoever can stand at the end of this gets the girl."

Before Ryn could agree, Lysyx lunged. Ryn landed hard on her back, Lysyx's weight on top of her. Pain erupted in Ryn's face as Lysyx landed two punches, one to her eye and one to her mouth. Spitting out blood, Ryn managed to throw Lysyx off.

Lysyx recovered first, though, and got her arm around Ryn's neck before Ryn could scramble to her feet. Lysyx tightened her hold. On her knees, Ryn coughed and clawed at the arm around her throat.

"Once I kill you," Lysyx growled, "how long do you think it'll take for the world to forget you? A day? An hour? You think your principles meant something, but all they got you was exile from the only place you ever called home."

Fury bubbled in Ryn's chest. She'd lost everything that day—her magic, her family, her life. But she'd rather be friendless on that lonely homestead than continue to bloody her hands in a senseless, unwinnable war.

She rammed her elbow into Lysyx's stomach. Lysyx didn't let go, but her grip loosened enough for Ryn to wriggle out of it. She kicked Lysyx in the chest, knocked her to the dusty ground, and slid the knife out of her boot. Kneeling, she plunged the knife into Lysyx's left palm.

Lysyx screamed, and then her screams turned into obscenities.

Breathing heavily, Ryn sat back on her haunches and regarded her old friend, someone she once thought of as a sister.

"Did it feel as good as you imagined?" Lysyx taunted, spittle flying from her lips. "All these nights, you've lain awake and dreamed of this moment. Are you satisfied, friend?"

Ryn licked her lips. Was she? In a heartbeat, she'd taken the magic of the woman who'd taken hers, and yet she felt no differently. She was still as empty as a dried-up well in a drought. She got to her feet, took a revolver from its holster, and aimed between Lysyx's eyes.

"No," she said.

And she pulled the trigger.

The conversations in the tavern ceased as soon as Ryn walked in. Unused to the attention, she inhaled and exhaled deeply to calm her racing heart. With her bruised and busted face and dirty clothing, she must look a fright.

Behind her, Nettie clomped her boots on the slatted floor to shake the dust off. She stepped up beside Ryn, their shoulders brushing. The contact, however light, knocked Ryn into action.

"We're here for the girl," she announced.

No one had to ask which.

Under the protection of a mesa, Gwyn lay down to sleep. Ryn watched her from across the fire. She had wanted to make it the whole way back to Lonesome by nightfall, but Gwyn was nine and she'd been through an ordeal and she was exhausted.

From her place next to Gwyn, Nettie studied Ryn's face. Quietly, she said, "Let's get you cleaned up."

"I'm fine," Ryn said.

Even though they'd kept their voices low, Gwyn sat up. She sloughed off her blanket, walked around the fire to where Ryn sat, and touched her cheek with her left hand. There was a question in her brown eyes. Terrified, Ryn nodded.

Gwyn released her magic. Ryn's breath caught, and she closed her eyes. She hadn't felt the touch of magic since her own had been taken from her. After all this time, she'd forgotten how calming it was. When she opened her eyes again, the pain had receded.

"Thank you," she said, her voice hoarse with emotion.

Gwyn smiled at her in the way only a child could smile, without deception or hidden motive, and she lay back down to sleep. After a moment or two, her breathing evened out.

Ryn watched her. She'd stay awake all night to watch over her. Nettie, who seemed to have the same idea, put a pot of water on the fire to boil for tea and then, blanket around her shoulders, sat next to her.

"Thank you," Nettie said softly. "I can't thank you enough for bringing her back to me."

Ryn didn't respond. She couldn't, not when it was so clear now that the only thing in the wide world she wanted was to be loved by family as fiercely as Nettie loved Gwyn.

Nettie took the pot off the fire and fixed up two cups of tea. She handed one to Ryn and, blanket over her shoulders, sat beside her. "Lysyx was the one who shot your hand, wasn't it?" she asked. "She took your magic."

Ryn's jaw tightened at the memory of them holding her down and pumping bullets into her palm as Lysyx watched. She'd been lucky they hadn't completely shredded the muscles. Only mostly. Though her hand hurt almost constantly, at least she could use it.

She sipped the tea, so hot it burned the top of her mouth. Strangely, she didn't feel the need to confirm Nettie's assumption aloud.

Nettie coaxed the cup out of Ryn's hand, pushed her gently to the ground, and covered her with a blanket. "Rest now. I'll keep watch."

Humphrey curled up in the pocket of her collarbone, and Ryn slept.

Back in Lonesome, Gwyn insisted on having Ryn stay for dinner, and because it was Gwyn, Ryn couldn't say no. So after their five siblings hugged Gwyn and Nettie tight, the eight of them squeezed around the dining table in the upper story of the tavern. The tavern, though small, served its purpose, which was to be a space for people to drink and forget, but this level left much to be desired. Everything from the two thin mattresses on the floor at one end to the beat-up table at the other spoke of there being too many people and too little room.

The kids didn't seem to mind. Alice and Xander, the oldest two, had made a fine supper of chicken, boiled potatoes, and asparagus. The younger ones were especially amused by Humphrey, who dashed around the room and leaped onto the furniture and the children. He seemed to be grateful to have an audience that wasn't Ryn's surly presence.

"I thought dragons were big!" said Ellian, the youngest boy.

"This is about as big as his species gets," Ryn said. "You gotta go north to see the big ones."

And his eyes went wide with excitement.

After supper, they had tea and sweet cakes while the kids, one by one, dropped off to sleep, Gwyn with her head in Ryn's lap. Surprisingly, she found she didn't mind the contact. Humphrey dozed near the hearth.

Nettie's eyes were drooping, too. Ryn should go soon, though there was one thing that had been bothering her all night.

"They're all war orphans?" she asked quietly.

Nettie answered with a nod.

"It's good of you to take care of them."

"We do what we can for family, even the ones we don't expect," Nettie said. "Alice was the first. I was already grown when she came to us."

Family. That was something Ryn had once. Here, in the glimmer of firelight, she thought it might be possible again. Cup in hand, she gestured around the room. "A bit small for so many of you."

Nettie smiled gently. "We get by. It's a better life than they would've had as orphans, and with them, my life is full instead of empty. Congestion comes with the territory."

Ryn cleared her throat. "It's just... My homestead's mighty big for just one person. Could use some extra hands with the animals, the crops. Be lots of room to sleep, to live."

"That's very kind," Nettie said, her gaze dropping, "but as crammed as we are in here, I couldn't bear to split the family up."

"You misunderstand. I wasn't suggesting splitting you up."

"You're thinking too much. You have to feel it," Ryn said as she crouched, hands on her knees, in front of Gwyn. The pasture spread wide around them.

"It's too hard," Gwyn said, looking discouraged.

"It is hard. It's gotta be. You don't use magic. You earn its trust, its companionship, and that takes time." Ryn bopped her chin. "That's it for tonight."

She sat down in the tall grass, and Gwyn followed suit. Ryn took off her hat, lay back, and watch the clouds meander across the darkening sky as the sun sank closer and closer to the horizon.

"What are we doing?" Gwyn whispered.

"Breathing," Ryn said. "Listening to the crickets. Watching the clouds. We're letting ourselves be."

"Because that's how the magic gets in?"

"Yeah," Ryn said, "that's how the magic gets in."

Soon, too soon, the dinner bell rang, and Gwyn raced back to the house. Ryn took one last deep breath, one last look at the sky. She put her hat back on as she traipsed through the long grass and smiled when Nettie greeted her at the door, part of the nightly routine.

"Smells delicious," Ryn said.

"Tastes delicious, too," Nettie said with a chuckle.

In the dining room, the entire family—for that was what they'd become—sat comfortably around the new table Ryn had made to accommodate them. With six kids, supper was a raucous affair, but Ryn found it preferable to the solitary quiet of her life before.

She even liked that it was her job to clean the table and the dishes while Nettie and the others sat in the parlor in the warmth of the fire playing games and telling stories. Humphrey, too, loved the new arrangement because it meant he got lots of attention all day long.

Once games were played and stories told and everyone retired for the night, Ryn sat at the edge of her mattress. With gentle, steady hands, Nettie wrapped her left palm in a cloth dampened with a tincture that smelled like peppermint. It was a human remedy, something Ryn had never heard of. The pain would recede and stay away until the following evening.

Once she'd tied off the bandage, Nettie smiled and said, "Rest now."

Ryn settled back on the bed, and she closed her eyes with no fear of nightmares.

The Journal
of Cutthroat Cass

Ryn stalked through the forest, her footsteps slow and measured. At her heels was Gwyn. After losing her magic—having it stolen by people she once called friends—Ryn hadn't wanted to think about it ever again. And she hadn't. Not until Gwyn was thrust into her life. Now she was teaching this young elf mage, a girl so like herself they could've been true siblings. Dark skin, dark eyes, lithe builds, and ears that slicked back into tiny points.

This was good for both of them, it seemed.

Ryn paused near a towering pine facing a clearing, went down on one knee, and put a reassuring hand on Gwyn's arm. "Remember what we practiced?"

Gwyn nodded solemnly. In that way, too, she was like Ryn. Serious and thoughtful, as though she carried the weight of the world on her shoulders at just nine years old.

The girl stepped into the clearing. Like Ryn had taught her, she closed her eyes, inhaled and exhaled deeply, letting all that tension from carrying the world go with it. She outstretched her left hand. This was the part where she cleared her mind and used her magic to reach out and sense what other life forms may be lingering in the trees. The trick was to quiet the mind so as not to let the sensations overwhelm it. Only then could you single out the bigger animals worth hunting, like deer, bison, or cougar. Though they'd practiced for only a morning, Ryn was confident her young charge could do this.

As she watched, Ryn's left palm tingled. She flexed her fingers, accustomed to moments like this, moments when she was so close to magic but could no longer feel it, could no longer bask in it. Still, being able to witness it was infinitely better than not being around it at all.

Another way Gwyn and her adopted siblings had unexpectedly blessed Ryn's life.

Gwyn opened her eyes. "This way," she said and headed into the forest.

Ryn followed at a short distance, letting her pupil take the lead.

Some four-hundred yards into their pursuit, the air changed, became heavy and thick, and Ryn's muscles tensed. As Gwyn's strides turned hesitant, Ryn caught up with her. She squinted through the trees, but fog had crept in, preventing her from seeing more than a few feet ahead. Even without magic, she could tell that there was something close by and that it was in pain.

She crept forward, step after tortured step. The loss of her magic had made her more attuned to the surrounding world. Now, she let the fog roll along with her, let it dictate her visibility. It was leading her, deliberately telling her to slow down, to calm down, to prepare herself for what was to come.

One more step, and the mist thinned enough to reveal the forest's secrets.

"Stop," Ryn said quietly, splaying a gentle hand across Gwyn's chest to halt her.

It was unnecessary. In a blink, Gwyn had already worked out that the creature was injured, and now she looked up at Ryn with concern.

"What is it?" she whispered.

"A peryton," Ryn said.

This one was a buck, his antlers stretching outward like bare winter branches. Majestic feathered wings sprouted from its deer-like body. Streaks of blood marred one of those wings and part of his torso. He stared at her with one large brown eye, seeming to take her measure.

Ryn frowned. Their kind wasn't common in these parts, and how had it been wounded?

"Go get your sister." Her voice was stern enough that Gwyn didn't have to guess which sister. The sister in charge, the one they all turned to in darkness.

Gwyn scampered off, back toward Lonesome, the town that lay in the valley beneath their homestead, where Nettie ran the tavern.

Ryn moved hesitantly toward the peryton, who flinched when she got too close. She held out a hand and murmured, "Don't worry. I won't hurt you."

At the wariness in its gaze, she sank to the soft dirt some distance away to wait for Nettie, who had turned out to be gifted when it came to rehabilitating wounded animals. Nowadays, she did more looking after the injured pegasi, calygreyhounds, and unicorns in the stables than Ryn did. With so many mouths to feed at the homestead, everyone had their tasks. It made for a full life, one Ryn hadn't expected to find. Perhaps the unexpectedness was partially why it contented her.

She sat silently, her gaze turned away from the peryton, hoping her presence was calming to the beast instead of frightening. They heard the approaching hoofbeats at the same time. The peryton twitched in fear, but she whispered, "Shh. She's here to help."

A moment later, Nettie trotted into view between the trees on her horse, Gwyn in front of her in the saddle. She halted a good ways away, dismounted almost soundlessly, and approached with caution.

When Nettie's gaze met hers, Ryn gave a nod of encouragement. Slowly, she rose to her feet and backed away as Nettie approached, one arm outstretched toward the peryton, who snorted anxiously.

"It's all right. You're all right," Nettie murmured, and when she touched the creature's neck, he closed his eyes and relaxed.

Ryn retreated to stand near Gwyn, still atop the horse, one reassuring hand on the girl's leg. Together, they watched Nettie, with patience and gentleness, treat the peryton's wounded wing.

After supper, Nettie found Ryn in her rocking chair on the front porch, wrapped in a thick blanket. Nettie sat on the adjacent chair, placed her lantern at their feet, and rubbed her eyes. She had coaxed the peryton into walking to the homestead, and they'd successfully installed him in a stall in the barn for the night. He could stay forever if he wanted to. The only thing Ryn couldn't figure out was how he'd gotten all the way out here in the first place.

Nettie sighed.

"Tired?" Ryn asked. She must be after the day she'd had. She poured a finger of whiskey into her empty glass and offered it to Nettie, who sipped and handed it back with mumbled thanks.

Ryn kept her boot heel on the porch boards as she rocked herself gently and gazed out at the dark land. It was peaceful out here, 'neath the stars, enough to chase away her nightmares of the war. Thankfully, those were rare now. She closed her eyes and felt the chilly breeze on her cheek. It was something—to be alive. Never thought she'd value that again.

After a little while, Nettie said, "Someone new came into the tavern today."

"Oh?"

"Said his name was Jediah Sloane."

Ryn stopped rocking. Damn.

"You know him?"

Ryn massaged her palm. The tincture she wrapped it in through the night was wearing off. "Know *of* him."

"That doesn't sound good."

Ryn worked her jaw, wished she had a cigar to smoke or a toothpick to chomp on. "He's a bounty hunter, a merciless one. Caught deserters in the war." She took a measured breath. "If he's here, it can't be for a good reason."

A shadow darted toward the barn.

Sitting up straighter, she squinted into the darkness. "What was that?"

Nettie whirled to follow her gaze. "What?"

Ryn grabbed the lantern and approached the shadow while Nettie disappeared inside. She held the light up in front of her, its bouncing beam flitting over a smallish humanoid shape.

"Hey!" she shouted and increased her pace.

The person tripped and hit the ground with an *oof.*

Nettie came racing out of the house to point her shotgun at his head. "Who the hell are you?"

He turned onto his rump and scrambled backward. "You have my peryton."

When Nettie let the barrel drop, he stopped trying to get away. His chest heaved.

"You can get up now," Ryn said.

His movements were sluggish and sloppy as he did so. Had he had too much to drink? He stepped into Ryn's light to reveal that he wasn't a man at all. At least, not a human one. He was a goblin.

And his shirt was coated in blood. Not drunk. Injured. Like his peryton.

"What happened to you?" she asked.

He pressed a hand to his side. "Let's just say there are some in these parts who object to my presence."

"Come on." Nettie gestured toward the house. "I can patch you up in there, and we have enough room for you for the night."

The goblin's face creased in confusion. "You'd help me? Why?"

"Someone helped me once. Meant the world to me," she said. "Figured I should pass that along when I can."

Ryn's cheeks heated, and she was grateful for the moonless night. She focused on the goblin's face, finding something familiar yet unreadable in his expression.

"Plog," he said, ambling after Nettie. "Plog is my name."

Ryn walked beside him with the lantern.

"Nice to meet you, Plog," Nettie said. "That's Ryn, I'm Nettie, and the children are sleeping, so we'll have to be quiet."

Inside, Nettie ushered Plog toward the kitchen table. Humphrey, Ryn's midnight-blue dwarf dragon, climbed onto the other end of the table to sniff curiously, but he made no move to come closer.

Grimacing, Plog removed his shirt, the gash in his side visible by the light of the lantern. A thin silvery scar marred half the length of his right arm.

Ryn filled a basin with water and set it nearby for Nettie. Then she gathered bandages, needles, and thread and waited to be of help. Nettie was good at this, though, taking care of people. Now, she cleaned Plog's wound with a soft, wet cloth, the water turning pink as she dipped it in the basin.

Nettie pointed to a needle. "Thread that for me, would you?"

Ryn complied, finding it difficult to knot the thin thread with her big fingers. Once she did, she handed it off.

Nettie looked at Plog with apprehension. "Are you ready?"

He gave a grim nod, but when she stuck the needle into his flesh to sew up the wound, a strangle cry emanated from his throat.

While Nettie paused, Ryn took off her belt and held it in front of Plog's mouth. "Here. Bite down on this."

He did so, Nettie plunged the needle in again, and this time, mercifully, he was quiet.

"What's going on?"

Too late. Alice, fourteen, stood in the doorway of the kitchen in her nightdress, almost like a spirit come to haunt them.

Ryn and the others looked toward her.

"Alice," Nettie said. "We didn't mean to wake you, but now that you're here, come help me wrap these bandages."

As Alice hurried to follow Nettie's instructions, Ryn felt an unexpected surge of pride. This one would grow up to be just like her big sister in all the best ways.

When it was done, Plog sat on the end of the sofa, wrapped in a blanket, a mug of tea in hand. Nettie sat beside him while Ryn took up a spot near the fireplace. Alice had fallen asleep in an armchair, Humphrey curled up in the warmth of her lap.

"I thank you for your kindness," Plog said between sips of tea, "but we'll have to be off in the morning."

"You won't get very far," Ryn said, "not like that."

"I agree. You need rest," Nettie said.

Plog raised one shoulder in a pained shrug. "Have to try."

"Why? Why are you here, and who doesn't want you here?" Ryn asked.

"I could ask the same of you. This is no man's land, a place for people who have nowhere to go. So, what are *you* doing here?"

"I don't think that's any concern of yours." Even under Plog's studious gaze, Ryn didn't flinch.

"You served in the war," said Plog, voice careful. "So did I."

Ryn let out a slow breath. So she *had* recognized that look in his eye, the one that said he'd seen too much and that it all weighed too heavily on him. "Not many of your kind were allowed to."

"No, not many."

"Which side?" Ryn asked, a challenge creeping into her tone. She didn't know what she wanted his answer to be, which would hurt worse. She wasn't exactly proud of the side she'd chosen.

His gaze flickered to Nettie then to Alice, the question clear in his eyes. An elf living with humans? Humans living with an elf? How odd it must look from the outside. No doubt he was wondering what the rest of the family looked like.

"Not that it matters, because neither side had any moral ground to stand on, but I fought for the humans for a while," he said.

For, not *with*. Interesting.

"All told, they're a little less prejudiced than elves," he said. "A little."

Ryn made a noncommittal noise in the back of her throat.

Nettie jumped in. "You still haven't explained why you're here or who's looking for you."

"Do you have anything stronger, by any chance?" Plog asked, holding out his teacup.

Ryn waited until her back was turned to roll her eyes, but she retrieved a bottle of whiskey and poured some into his tea. When he didn't take the cup back, she added another splash and set the bottle on the mantle.

Plog tipped the cup and swallowed the concoction in two big gulps.

Before he could open his mouth to speak, Nettie said, "It's Jediah Sloane, isn't it?"

Plog nodded. "'Fraid so."

"Why's he after you?" asked Ryn.

"He's not after me, not technically. He's after something I've got."

Ryn's irritated response was cut off by a look from Nettie, who leaned toward Plog. "What is it, and why is it so important?" Ever the more tactful one.

"A journal." Plog hesitated, gaze focused on the rug. "Belonged to Cutthroat Cass."

Nettie looked questioningly to Ryn, who said, "She was a mercenary in the war. Half-elf, half-dwarf. Got the best attributes from both lines, too."

"D'you ever see her fight?" asked Plog.

Ryn shook her head. She'd only heard stories.

Plog whistled. "It was something, all right. Never thought something so deadly could be so beautiful."

"Why is her journal so important?" asked Nettie.

"She had two weapons—a sword from the dwarves and a gun from the elves. Both were said to possess magical qualities, and after watching her fight, I can't say I disagree," Plog said.

"And her journal contains—or is thought to contain—the secrets of these weapons and her own fighting ability?"

Plog tipped his head. "Just so. Besides that, there's just bad blood between her and Sloane. Never got the full story, though."

"Where is she now? That you're the one delivering her journal?"

"Went into hiding after the war. Too many people wanted what she had," Ryn said. "Lots of people said she'd died, but as none of them could settle on *how* she died, I wasn't inclined to believe them."

"Oh, she's out there somewhere, bidin' her time," Plog agreed.

Ryn considered what, exactly, she was biding her time for. If Cass felt anything like Ryn did after the war, the path she'd choose next would atone for her sins during it.

"Where are you meant to deliver the journal to?" Nettie asked.

"Shadowedge."

"Well, then, it's settled," said Nettie.

"How d'you mean?" asked Plog.

"Shadowedge is only a day and a half away at most, or so I've heard. You *and* your mount are injured, and you're in need of an escort to protect you from Sloane. Ryn and I can offer that. Do you not agree?" Nettie, looking between Ryn and Plog, smiled. "So, that's that. We leave in the morning."

"Be good," Nettie said as she squeezed Moss so tight he was turning red. "And all of you, you're to listen to Alice and Xander, all right?"

Ryn said goodbye to each of the kids and offered Humphrey, who was perched on Gwyn's shoulder, a scratch on the head. He leaned into her palm.

"When will you come home?" Gwyn asked in a small voice.

"Soon," said Ryn.

The elf child wouldn't look at her, and tears threatened.

A hand on her free shoulder, Ryn led her a ways apart from the others. She squatted in front of her to look her in the eyes. "We have to help people when we're able. You and your sister taught me that. I know you're worried about us, and it's all right to be worried. But . . ." She paused, licked her lips because her mouth was too dry to go on. "But I promise you we're both coming home. I promise."

Gwyn gave one solid nod to convey her understanding.

Ryn kissed her on the forehead and walked over to the cart, to which both their horses were hitched. She climbed up in the front beside Nettie. On the cart's straw-filled pallet lay Plog and the peryton, both tucked up in blankets and both, within the first half-hour of the journey, asleep.

Nettie glanced back and then said quietly, "You're worried."

"I'm always worried," said Ryn.

A tiny smile. "Yes, but when you're *especially* worried, the wrinkle in your forehead deepens even more. So, what is it?"

Ryn sighed. "If Jediah is any good at his job, which he is, he'll be following us."

"I know."

"I don't want to have to kill him."

"I know."

She'd killed Lysyx all those months ago. But that had been different, hadn't it? Lysyx had been the past she couldn't run from, and she'd put that to bed because she'd had to. This was different, and, to tell truth, she was afraid of what she might do. Or what she might not be able to stop herself from doing.

"You protect the weak. Sometimes, that means defeating the strong. No one can fault you for that, not even yourself," said Nettie. She placed her hand on Ryn's arm. "But since you will, whatever happens, remember you don't have to do this alone. You don't have to *bear* it alone."

They set up camp for the night at the summit of a hill. After supper, Plog ushered the peryton into the cart to bed down and then climbed in after him. Nettie lay on her bedroll in the grass, but her rifle was beside her and she wouldn't fall asleep. Ryn took comfort in that as she climbed onto a rock to keep watch, a blanket around her shoulders and her pistol clutched in one hand.

Above, clouds blotted out most of the stars. Funny how they shone down on everyone the same—good or bad, moral or immoral. Her thoughts turned to Sloane. Bounty hunting was as respectable a profession as any other, and often, they were responsible for bringing bad men to justice, but a man like Jediah Sloane wasn't ever going to be respectable and he didn't care about justice. He wasn't going to let innocent people like Plog live their quiet lives. There was only one way to deal with a man like that, one way to stop him from hunting anyone else. She wouldn't relish doing it, and the decision was a heavy one, but making it relaxed her tense body. She had a purpose, and it was that purpose she focused on.

He came after midnight, when Ryn's joints were stiff with cold. Ready nonetheless, she jumped from the rock to place herself between him and his sleeping prey.

"Stand aside," said Jediah Sloane. "My quarrel ain't with you."

"Actually, it is." Ryn aimed her pistol at his head, right between his eyes.

"Aw, you don't want to use that, sweetheart. Don't want to wake him, after all."

Ryn snarled, and she was about to protest the nickname when, behind Sloane, Nettie rose from her bedroll and aimed her rifle at his heart. Ryn briefly met her gaze, took comfort in the fact that Nettie had spoken true—she wasn't alone, and she didn't have to bear it like she was.

"Just give me the journal, and I'll be on my way."

She wanted to blast the smarmy grin off his face, but first, she needed information. "Who are you working for?" Because that was what it came down to, didn't it? A bounty hunter didn't have a job unless someone was paying him, and she had to be sure that someone wasn't interested in instigating another conflict, no matter the scale.

He stepped into her space. "You don't have to worry about that."

"I don't," she said, "but I will."

She squeezed the trigger, but he snagged her wrist and the shot went wide. His punch landed on her jaw, knocking her back a few steps. She shook off the pain, spat out the blood, and fought his grip on her wrist. When she got free, she'd blow his brains out.

With a sneer, he said, "You've stepped into something you don't understand, girl. Not every man would be as for—"

Nettie swung the butt of her rifle into his skull, dropping him to the ground. "Men," she said, exasperated. "They always talk so much."

And Ryn, breathing heavily in relief, felt the weight slough from her bones.

The afternoon sun beat down upon them as they trundled their way toward an enormous mesa. Ryn walked alongside the cart now, holding the rope that led to Sloane's tied hands. The roughness of the strands under her palms reminded her of the life she held. She could still kill him. She could do it with a bullet through his brain or just by tying him up and leaving him here to dehydrate in the middle of the desert.

Her gaze flicked to Plog and his peryton, resting in the back of the cart, and to Nettie, sitting up front and driving. Ryn had killed in the war, of course, under orders, and she had killed Lysyx in retaliation for stealing her magic. Last night, though, if it hadn't been for Nettie, Ryn was sure she would've killed again, and it wouldn't have been absolutely necessary. What did that say about her?

Her stomach roiled as she dwelled on it, so she pushed it from her mind just as they approached an archway cut into the side of the mesa and stopped in front of it.

"The community's inside?" Nettie asked curiously. "How very interesting."

Plog ambled out of the cart gingerly. "Something like that."

With Nettie's help, he coaxed out the peryton, too, and they led the way into the depths of the mesa. Ryn made to follow when the rope pulled taut. Behind her, Sloane had planted his heels in the dust and was resisting her momentum.

"I ain't going in there," he said and spat on the ground.

"Fine." She pushed him against the rock wall, maneuvered him into a sitting position, and tied his ankles. Without a second glance, she turned to catch up with her friends.

Inside, a wide tunnel led to a large round room lighted by two braziers. In the center of the room was a cage on a raised platform.

Plog led his peryton up the steps and into the enclosure. He looked at them expectantly. "Come on, then."

Nettie climbed up without hesitation or fear, and Ryn followed her. She was coming to the conclusion that it was generally smart to follow Nettie's lead. Once they were in, Plog closed the door and pulled a lever. There was a *hiss* of steam from somewhere above, and then the platform began to rise. Though the movement was slow, Ryn grasped onto the bars to steady herself.

"What's . . . happening?" Nettie asked, gaze pointed upward.

"It's a lift," said Plog. "Don't worry. It's perfectly safe."

Ryn pursed her lips as a noise escaped her throat. It was an odd sensation, but if the peryton wasn't bothered, she shouldn't be, either.

After another minute or so, the cage emerged into the sunlight and came to a halt. Plog unlatched the door, and they stepped out into the middle of a town.

"They're with me," Plog said to the waiting guard, a human woman with close-cropped hair and a gnarled nose.

"This," Nettie said breathlessly as Plog led them through the streets, "is incredible. How long have you lived up here? Is it sustainable? Where do you get your water? From the rainfall? Is there enough of it?"

Far from being bothered by the ceaseless questions, Plog seemed pleased. Was this his home, then? And if so, how long had it been his home? He answered Nettie with equal enthusiasm, but Ryn paid little attention and instead surveyed the town. The streets were laid out at neat angles. Near the center of the town were the public buildings and attractions—the courthouse, a theater, saloons, even a hotel. As they walked, the structures became private homes, and past those, she could even see pasture, with cows and sheep and horses roaming. As Nettie had said, incredible.

Plog brought them to a narrow, two-story house with a front porch that overlooked a gated postage stamp of a garden in which milkvetch, thistle, and capeweed grew. He closed the gate behind them and let the peryton lie down in the shade.

The front door opened before Plog could knock, revealing a tall, broad woman in a loose shirt over large biceps, britches and suspenders, and soft boots. Thick, curly brown hair was pulled back from her face, her pointy ears visible.

Cutthroat Cass.

Ryn raised an irritated eyebrow and muttered, "You didn't say you were delivering Cass's journal *to* her." He'd given the impression he'd been tasked with handing it off *from* Cass to her family or close friends.

"Didn't say I wasn't, either," Plog replied smugly.

Cass greeted him with a hug. "Old friend," she said, "it is good to have you back." Her voice, a mixture of honey and gravel, was oddly comforting.

"And it's good to see your face again. This is Nettie and Ryn. They patched me up and helped me get here to give you this. " He retrieved the journal from his satchel and held it out to her.

"Thank you for bringing it," said Cass to all three of them. She ran her fingers over the worn cover. "It means a lot to me and contains information that should not fall into unsavory hands."

"There's something else," Nettie said.

"This is quite the gift already."

Plog grinned. "We've brought you Sloane."

Ryn sat on the top step of the front porch, breathing in the cool night air. With a number of Cass's associates joining the table, dinner had been large and pleasant, but Nettie was so much better at things like that. Sighing, she flexed her left hand. Nettie had been sure to pack the balm she needed, but she hadn't yet applied it tonight. She would have to before she went to sleep.

The door creaked open, and Cass settled down beside her. She leaned back on her elbows, stretched her legs out down the steps, and crossed them at the ankles. "You, my friend, have delivered me something of great value as well as dropped one of my enemies into my hands. Yet you're out here all alone."

Ryn lifted a shoulder. "Noise bothers me sometimes."

"Is that all that's bothering you?" When Ryn stiffened, Cass added, "I know a fellow veteran when I see one, and if you're anything like me, the nightmares are hard to chase away, especially after you come across a man such as Jediah Sloane. Not an honorable bone in his body."

Ryn looked out at the town, encased in darkness, then up at the stars. Though she'd known Cass for only a few hours, if she couldn't tell her, then who? "I would've killed him. I'd made up my mind to do it."

"And did you?"

"No."

"Why not?"

"Nettie . . . found another way. She was the one who suggested bringing him to you."

"Then why do you fret?"

"Because if she hadn't been there, I would have done it. She *was* there, and I still wanted to. If it weren't for her, I'd have more blood on my hands."

Cass let that confession sit for a long while. Then she said, "Doing monstrous things doesn't necessarily make us monsters."

"No?" Ryn said humorlessly. "What does it make us?"

"Survivors," Cass said. "And protectors. This world is harsh, and there are countless people who would take advantage of others' weakness. Perhaps we can't entirely make up for our past sins, but protecting those who can't protect themselves doesn't make us wicked."

Ryn sighed. She knew she wasn't wicked, not like Sloane. But she wasn't golden like Nettie and Gwyn and the rest, either. What did that make her, then?

Cass sat up and waited for Ryn to look her way. "People like you and me—we will always have demons. And sometimes, when we fall and our demons take hold of us, the ones we protect will be there to protect us. That's not weakness. Having people who love us that much—that's true strength."

The words were so similar to Nettie's from the previous day that Ryn had to consciously catch her breath. Hadn't that, in a way, been the driving force behind inviting Nettie and her siblings to live on the homestead? Because when she was alone, she hadn't felt strong. She'd felt lost and empty. But when she was with them, Gwyn especially, the days didn't seem so bleak, the nights so dark.

"Remember that," Cass said kindly, "next time you bloody your hands. Remember the people you bloody them for, and remember to ask for help in washing them off." She patted Ryn's shoulder then rose and went back inside, where Nettie and Plog and the others waited.

Ryn took a moment to close her eyes and breathe in deeply. No, she wasn't as good or as just as Nettie was, but she wouldn't stop trying to walk the path of justice. Now that she had a family to redirect her when she faltered, walking it didn't seem so difficult.

With a final glance at the stars, she joined the others inside.

Other books by Carrie Gessner

The Heartfriends Series:
The Dying of the Golden Day
The Shadow of the Endless Night

The Stroke of Thirteen

The stories found in this collection that can also
be found online or in anthologies are:

"Creatures of the Night Shift" - *Work In Progress*
"How You Find It" - *Whispers in the Dark*
"Lonesome" - *Gunsmoke & Dragonfire*
"The Offerings" - *Freeze Frame Fiction*
"The Planet of Purple Forests" - *Beautiful Lies,
Painful Truths Vol. 1*
"Steeping Spells" - *Fall Into Fantasy 2018*
"A Whisper from the Waves" - *The Future Fire*